ALSO BY DE'SHAWN CHARLES WINSLOW

In West Mills

Decent People

THE FERVENT WHITES

THE FERVENT WHITES

A NOVEL

DE'SHAWN CHARLES WINSLOW

ONE WORLD
NEW YORK

One World
An imprint of Random House
A division of Penguin Random House LLC
1745 Broadway, New York, NY 10019
oneworldlit.com
penguinrandomhouse.com

Hardcover ISBN 9780593977910
Ebook ISBN 9780593977927

Printed in the United States of America

1st Printing

First Edition

BOOK TEAM:
Production editor: Loren Noveck
Managing editor: Allison Fox
Production manager: Sandra Sjursen
Copy editor: Bonnie Thompson
Proofreaders: Cyrus Chin, Kyndle Fuller, and Robin Slutzky

Book design by Edwin A. Vazquez

The authorized representative in the EU for product safety and compliance is Penguin Random House Ireland, Morrison Chambers, 32 Nassau Street, Dublin D02 YH68, Ireland. https://eu-contact.penguin.ie

To the reader, once again

THE FERVENT WHITES

CHAPTER ONE

JUNE 1982

The triplet of knocks came from the front door just as Sylvia Upshaw and her two children were putting on their shoes, about to walk over to Mrs. Talbot's house. Syl's daughter, GiGi, her first-born, peered through the living room window, which looked out onto their small front lawn.

"It's the Whites," she said.

"The Whites? James and Ella White?" Syl asked. A sudden pang of fear fluttered in her stomach.

Then Syl's son, RJ, had a look. "What the—" RJ said, his eyes fixed on their unexpected guests.

Syl shooed her teens away from the window and glanced out herself. There they stood, James and Ella White, her fresh-out-of-prison neighbors. James was rocking back and forth on his heels. Ella stood still, wearing what Syl might describe as a half-smile. James stretched his neck and winced. Everyone in the hamlet of Fervent—in all of Saugerties, and maybe even in the whole Hudson Valley—knew they had been released from prison a week ago. But no one had expected them to return to the neighborhood.

The two of them stood on Syl's porch, which in actuality was just a wide, square block of cement. Only one of Syl's kitchen chairs could fit. Syl had asked her ex-husband to build a *real* porch so that they could sit out on it together, but he never got around to it. He had been too busy getting around to other women's needs.

"I've never spoken to *murderers* before," RJ whispered, towering over Syl and GiGi.

"You won't speak to any today, either, dummy," GiGi shot back. "They're innocent, remember?"

"You know what I meant."

"Hush, both of you," Syl ordered. "Stand over there." She pointed to a far corner of their living room where a bookshelf hosted forty or fifty paperbacks—romances, mysteries, and thrillers.

"Ma, open the door. You're being rude."

"Quiet, GiGi," she whispered, pointing again to the corner. GiGi hesitated—a new but subtle defiance the girl had begun showing in recent weeks, now that she was a rising high school senior. RJ, a year younger than his sister, would soon follow suit, Syl imagined.

Before heading to the door, Syl looked out the window at the Whites' hands. The rippling in her stomach got quicker by the second. She saw no weapons or anything that could be used as one. Syl used her foot to move the old beach towel she had tucked at the bottom of the door. June was three-quarters gone and summer was in full swing. They had been running the window unit for a couple of weeks. Most of the houses in Fervent leaked air; no matter how hard the owners tried to keep the cool in, it found its way out. Back in '73, Syl had inherited the house, and its problems and its mortgage, from her great-aunt.

Syl opened the heavier inner door and wondered if the glass storm door that separated her from the Whites reminded them of receiving visitors at Bedford Hills and Attica. Given how close Syl and her children had been to the Whites' son—Morgan had been one of the kindest, most dependable people in the hamlet—

she also wondered how they felt about never receiving visits or even a letter from her.

"Sylvia," Ella said, head tilted just a little to one side. Ella never called her *Syl,* like everyone else. "It's so good to see you." The flutter in Syl's gut was now annoyance at what she suspected was phoniness coming from Ella.

"Ella. James," Syl said, folding her arms just under her breasts. "I didn't know you two were back in Saugerties."

The Whites donned what may have been genuine smiles—given their newfound freedom. They weren't cursing Syl or daring her to come out and face them. *Do they know I told their secret while they were in prison?* she wondered.

Most of Ella's hair was gone. Cut short, like the lady's haircut in *Rosemary's Baby.* Syl couldn't remember the lead actress's name. Ella must have made the change in the past few days, because last week, when Syl saw the short clip of her speaking at the news conference—it aired live while Syl was at work—her light blond hair was pulled back in the ponytail she was known for. Syl was surprised by how much she liked Ella's striking new look.

With far less hair, Ella's green eyes seemed greener, like those of the feral black cats that roamed their hamlet, meowing for table scraps, which were often given without hesitation. Ella was wearing a pair of dark blue denims, and the color of her button-up blouse made Syl want honeydew melon. Ella had always been a petite woman, but now she looked strong, her jawline more pronounced, her forearms rippling.

James, who was much taller than his wife, was also wearing new-looking denims, along with a plain white T-shirt. James had let his hair grow to his shoulders, about the same length as Syl's. But it was no longer the mostly-pepper-and-some-salt it had been when he and Ella went to prison early last year. Now it was mostly salt.

He had put on some heft, Syl observed, and from the way his shirt hugged him, it seemed like all muscle—the blue veins in his forearms more visible, more threatening, than before.

But he's not a murderer, Syl, remember.

James, a military veteran—he'd served in Vietnam—had always been fit. He was accustomed to rigorous, vigorous daily exercise. It was nothing to see him jogging around the hamlet's one oval-shaped street. In the winter, when the trees were bare, Syl could see straight down to the riverbank where James sometimes went to do his jumping rope and other exercises Syl never knew the names for. Just as common was to see James doing pull-ups on basketball hoops over in town, or push-ups against the cold pavement of the parking lot at Aco, Inc., the toy factory where she worked.

It was also where James had worked before Paul Hope was killed.

"Sorry to drop by unannounced like this. We tried to call from Mrs. Talbot's, but the line was busy," Ella said. GiGi had been on the phone for the past hour, the receiver tucked between her head and her left shoulder, a Prince album playing loudly so Syl couldn't hear her gossiping. Syl liked Prince, and she was especially taken by the second cut on that record, "Sexuality." Still, Syl didn't think it needed to be blasted to be enjoyed. "I told James we may as well just knock and see, since we saw your car."

Syl couldn't believe they had gone to Mrs. Talbot's. Syl knew how her neighbors could be. Curt and Patrice "Peaches" Bainbridge had probably greeted the Whites but avoided them after that—too proud to admit they'd been wrong. Ervin and Suzy John were likely to have gone into Mrs. Talbot's bathroom and prayed for everyone's safety. Mark and Belinda Fleming likely treated the Whites as though they were Farrah Fawcett and Ryan O'Neal. And if Hoke Robinson was there, he probably shook their hands, welcomed them back to Fervent, and left. He wasn't a big fan of James's, but he, too, had always believed they were innocent of Paul Hope's murder.

Ella explained that when they'd passed Mrs. Talbot's house on their way to their own—they had borrowed a car from James's uncle, down in the city—they'd noticed the balloons tied to Mrs. Talbot's door and the cars parked out front. So they'd stopped to see what was going on.

Syl's face must have betrayed her, because James said, "We know, we know. You guys weren't expecting us to move back here so soon after getting out."

If Syl had thought there was the slightest chance that James and Ella would ever be released from prison, she would have never sat Morgan down and told him the secret she had sworn to keep. As she stood there, looking at the Whites, she felt as though the guilt would chew her out of existence. She wanted James and Ella gone, away from her door.

Ella fanned herself with her hand.

"Sylvia, do you have a few minutes?"

If GiGi and RJ hadn't been there, Syl might have told Ella no and asked the Whites not to return to her home. But the children would later accuse her of being rude, and they'd certainly ask questions she didn't want to answer. So Syl opened the door, stepped aside, and invited them in.

CHAPTER TWO

Once the Whites were both inside, Syl extended her hand to Ella, expecting only a quick, firm shake. But Ella pulled Syl to her and held on tight for several seconds. Then James came in for a hug, smelling of cigarette smoke—a habit he had quit some years ago but must have picked back up in prison. It all felt strange to Syl, being embraced by the couple. But under the circumstances, allowing their hugs was the neighborly thing to do—not only because they'd been released from prison after eighteen months, but because they'd lost their only child and never got to say goodbye to him. At Morgan's funeral, Mrs. Talbot—who had lost her husband five months prior—delivered the eulogy. Syl's best friend, Fate—also a Fervent resident—sang a hymn.

Syl had never been close to the Whites. In fact, she had always been skeptical of them—a white couple with an adopted Black son. It all reminded her of the McLaughlin family back in her hometown of Elizabeth City, North Carolina. The McLaughlin couple adopted their maid's son after his mother was abruptly taken by pneumonia. In Syl's opinion, the McLaughlins turned him against Black people. She often wondered what ever happened to Clyde, whose name was changed to Claude after the adoption.

Syl understood that Ella knew Morgan's birth mother, but

she had never thought it was right. "Black kids should be raised in Black homes. And James and Ella seem—I don't know—not very comfortable around Black folk. Especially James," she had told her husband when they first met the Whites. Still, she worked with James and committed herself to being neighborly with everyone in the hamlet.

But she loved Morgan, who was like a nephew to her and an older cousin to her children. He shared Atari games with RJ and showed him how to pop wheelies on his bicycle. With GiGi, Morgan talked poetry and answered her questions about the older boys with whom he had classes. And because he had such a steady hand, he would even paint GiGi's fingernails when Syl wasn't in the mood to smell the polish.

"If you ever become a dad to daughters, you'll treat them like princesses, Morgan," Syl had heard GiGi tell him as he layered burnt-orange polish onto her daughter's nails.

"Can't argue with that," Morgan had replied. "I plan to spoil my wife and all my children—when I have them. But, yeah, my girls will be spoiled rotten."

Syl said, "Welcome back, you two. And I'm so, so sorry for your loss. I should've said that first. We miss Morgan so much around here."

Just saying Morgan's name brought forth a wave of pain. Syl sometimes found herself awake at night, tossing and turning, pacing her bedroom, then sitting at her old, paint-longing vanity, looking at Morgan's face on the newspaper clipping that had announced his death to the people of Saugerties. For the first few weeks, she'd stayed up listening to GiGi's sobbing through their bedroom walls, wishing she could inhale the secret back in.

"Welcome back, Miss Ella and Mr. James," GiGi said. "I like your haircut, Miss Ella."

"Thank you, gorgeous," Ella replied. "A new day, a new look, I suppose. It's funny. Many of the other ladies in that awful place got their hair cut every chance they had. I didn't. But when James and I got to his mother's apartment the other day, it was one of the first things I did. On a whim I said, 'Why not?'" She turned to Syl. "I'm glad I did it, Sylvia. It feels freeing. I cried so many tears into my hair while in that place. Tears over Morgan's death, tears for being there, tears for no one believing in our innocence. The hair had to go. Come here, you two. Hugs." Syl signaled to her kids that it was okay.

The hair had to go, Ella had just said. It reminded Syl of a conversation—it had turned into an argument—in which she and Reggie had offered to take Morgan along with them to RJ's haircuts. The Whites had been taking Morgan to the same man who cut James's hair. Not knowing how to handle a Black person's hair, the barber most often simply buzzed all of Morgan's hair off.

"Thanks, you two," Ella had said from behind her screen door. "But we've got it under control. We don't have to be Black to understand there are different types of haircuts for our Black son. We like the buzz-cut look for him, and *he* likes it."

"The kids are saying he's complaining about it, though," Syl had said. "We just thought we'd offer you—"

"Come on, Syl," Reggie had said, gently pulling her away from the Whites' porch. "None of our business."

"I don't mean to be rude, Sylvia, but your husband's right," Ella said. "This has probably ruined my day, if I'm honest."

"Ruined your day? Because a *Black* mother is offering some help with your *Black* son?"

"Syl," Reggie said.

"If that's going to ruin your day, you need to figure out why."

"I'm going to close my door now, Sylvia. I know—I *hope* you meant well. But no thanks."

Now Syl watched Ella embrace GiGi and RJ.

"Many of us believed in your innocence, Ella," Syl asserted. It came out more defensively than she had intended. But the statement was at least half true.

"Oh, we know, Syl," James said in his staccato way. He palmed Syl's left shoulder and rapidly squeezed it twice.

"I didn't mean that *no one* believed us," Ella clarified. She rested a palm on Syl's right shoulder. "But thank you for saying that. Really."

Well, if they know I told their secret, they're being awfully forgiving, Syl reflected. *Or are they not bringing it up because the kids are here?*

"Yeah, we're pretty glad the truth is out," RJ chimed in.

Ella blushed and gazed down at her white tennis shoes, which looked fresh from the box. It was obvious to Syl that the Whites hadn't heard many comforting words since their arrests. "We're glad Josey and Foust confessed," James began, his voice an octave higher than it had been a few minutes ago. Syl wondered if it was an attempt to change the tone of the room. But then he said, "Those are two crazy motherfu—"

"James," Ella cut in.

"Man, those guys are messed up in the head." He swept his fingers through his hair. "I guess he decided that if he was going in for the rest of his life, he might as—"

"James, please," Ella said, looking up at him sternly. Syl shared Ella's sentiment.

"Well, we'd still be locked up, for life, if he hadn't confessed. Shit. We—"

"We're trying not to think too much about what that future would've looked like, remember?" Ella broke in. "The time we *did* spend in those prisons will haunt us enough." Her eyes watered. James put his arm around her shoulders and kissed the top of her head, his hair falling and covering her face. "God, I wish our boy was here to welcome us home. I don't know how I'm going to handle his absence, Sylvia," she added. "I just don't know how I'm going to do it."

Syl felt a wail of sorrow and immense guilt moving from her abdomen up into her chest. But she was able to hold it in.

"It won't be easy," Syl said to Ella. "But you're strong. Both of you are. I'm so sorry you two went through—everything. All of it is just terrible. I'm so sorry." And she was. Sincerely. She crossed her arms, then dropped them to her sides. "Like RJ said, we're glad the truth is out."

The truth was, for most of their speedy trial, Syl had been on the fence about whether or not they were guilty. James had taken lives in combat, Syl had long ago learned from the late Mr. Talbot. He was more than capable.

"Thank you, Syl," James said.

"I didn't expect you two to come back here to Saugerties," Syl said, surprising herself. "So soon, I mean. Anyway, I'm glad that you're free, but we just thought—"

"Who's we? You and Fate?" James asked, and Syl frowned. "I'm just teasin'. I know you two are thick as thieves." He patted her shoulder again.

"Everyone. Here in Fervent, at least," Syl said.

"We're not interested in moving anyplace else and starting from scratch. Not at our ages, Sylvia."

"We're getting long in the tooth, us two," James added. "And this is Morgan's restin' place. So—"

"This is still home for us," Ella said.

Morgan was buried in the small public cemetery that shared a ditch with Richmont's Petro. Ella's chin dropped to her chest and she closed her eyes tight, as though trying to hold back tears, or maybe a scream. Syl noticed Ella's deepened crow's-feet. *The things time and sadness do to us,* she thought.

"We understand why people would think that, but we *love* Saugerties and you all here in Fervent," Ella said. "We know there'll always be a bit of stain on our names. People don't forget scandal. But this is our *community.* So, we're not going *any*where."

"I guess we oughta get to the point of why we stopped by," James said. "We came to say we know what you and Fate did, Syl." He slid both hands in his pockets, and his jaw tightened. "And we won't forget it."

Syl began to feel as though she were standing in front of a hot brick oven. She was two seconds away from screaming to her kids to run when she took a step back and nearly tripped on the edge of the area rug.

"Whoo-oops," Ella said in a singsong tone. She caught Syl by both arms and prevented the fall. Ella's quick reflexes were unnerving. "Are you okay, dear?"

"Yeah," Syl said. "Thanks. I'm alright. I need to move this old rug."

Ella rubbed Syl's upper arm and said, "Sylvia, I shouldn't have been surprised when Morgan told me in a letter. He didn't write many."

Letter? Syl thought. *Told you what? Dear God in heaven.*

"You were so *kind* to him while we were away," Ella continued. Syl felt her shoulders relax, but she was unable, unwilling to allow her eyes to meet Ella's.

"Well, I just—"

"Come on, Syl," James said. "Come on. It wasn't *just* anything. Don't sell yourself short. We really appreciate it. Mo did, too." Syl had forgotten that James had given Morgan that nickname. In fact, James was the only one who sometimes called Morgan *Mo.*

"Well," Syl said, "we, Fate and I, just wanted to make sure he ate well and all. You know young people'll eat cereal and fast food all day, if you don't stop them. He probably thought Fate and I overstepped—at first, at least." Syl often wanted to overstep, more than she had when Morgan was a child.

"Overstepped?" Ella said, tilting her head to the left. "I don't think he thought that at all. Not one bit, Sylvia."

"He probably did a little bit, in the beginning," James said with a raspy chuckle.

Ella, looking straight into Syl's eyes, said, "We're grateful, Sylvia. *Beyond* grateful. You didn't have to do that while raising your own two. Morgan was a grown man. Young, but a man. But you knew him well enough to know that twenty years on this earth doesn't always make someone a grown-up."

"He loved the three of you," James said, gesturing to Syl and her children. Syl could tell they didn't want to talk about Fate. She wasn't surprised they didn't acknowledge Fate's involvement in looking in on Morgan.

They don't know what I told Morgan, she thought. *I'd know by now.*

Syl's quivering lips and trembling hands had calmed, so she took a deep breath and offered the pair her condolences again.

"I'm sorry Morgan's not with us right now" was all she could think to say. She didn't say what she often thought, which was: if she hadn't told Morgan about his birth parents, he might still be alive.

At the time, she felt it made perfect sense for Morgan to know the truth. The Whites had been tried and convicted for Hope's murder, never to be free again. The guilt Syl carried about not sharing with Morgan the information he had every right to learn had kept her up at night. She had believed it was time for the young man to know.

Fate had told her time and time again that Morgan's death was not her fault.

"You didn't force Morgan to go on that trip, Syl," Fate had said, moving from his rose-colored velvet armchair to sit next to her on the matching couch. "I won't hear you blame yourself for this anymore."

Now the Whites were standing in her living room thanking her for loving their late son. It all felt crazy.

"Listen, Syl, I'll be honest with ya. Fate said a *little* more than we liked on the witness stand," James said, holding up his thumb and index finger, about a quarter of an inch between the two. "But we know he was only answering the prosecutor's questions. He didn't mean any harm. At least, I *hope* he didn't mean us any harm."

Ella glanced over at GiGi and RJ. A motherly desire to protect them from negativity, Syl supposed. Then, to Syl, Ella said, "All water under the bridge."

"Fate really *didn't* mean any harm," Syl said, thinking about the past animosity between Fate and the Whites. "None of us did. Like you said, James. We just answered the questions."

During the trial, which had commenced in December of 1981 and concluded the very next month, Fate broke under the pressure of the prosecutor's questions and mentioned a couple of hiccups he and the Whites had once had. It didn't look good at all for James, who, back in '79, had gotten physical with Fate. And it didn't bode well for Ella that she had basically cheered James on. Though they had apologized to Fate for that terrible business, Fate hadn't really forgiven them. How was he supposed to? If the insults were water under the bridge, Fate kept his eyes on the Whites from the top of it.

"We hope to see Fate within the next day or so," Ella said. "He wasn't at Mrs. Talbot's." Ella finally seemed to notice that

Syl's pocketbook was hanging from her shoulder. "Well, it looks like you all were headed out, so we'll go. Are you heading to the celebration? I'm so proud of her. Her very first sale as a real estate agent. She's been wanting to find something new to do for years."

"We're headed over there right now. I bet seeing you two made her smile." *Or maybe it ruined the party.*

"She's having a ball," James said, with a big smile. "And you know what, Syl. She deserves it, especially with Mr. T up and passing away. Gosh, I miss that old man already, and I just drove back to Fervent. He wrote me once a month while I was in there. Great man."

They all nodded to that. While Syl believed a Black boy needed a Black father, she would have approved of the late Mr. Grant Talbot, the oldest white man in Fervent, being a dad to Morgan.

"We should go, James, so they can get to the party," Ella said, nudging him. "We'll be seeing you, Sylvia. Bye, kids. Oh, listen to me calling you *kids.* You've grown so tall in the past year and a half, both of you. Tall like your father. What are your plans for the summer?"

"They're going down south to him," Syl said, trying to give the short answer before RJ had a chance to list all the things his father and stepmother had planned for them in Atlanta. "I'm putting them on the train in a few days."

The moment Syl spoke the word *train,* she wanted to rewind life's cassette. But it was too late. Ella had already winced.

"Oh, it's a shame you'll be gone," Ella said. "We're going to do a little memorial walk for Morgan in a week or so. On that hiking trail he loved. We're inviting everyone here in Fervent, keeping it small."

"Oh?" Syl said.

"But you two know the trail and you've probably already been there to think about him," James said to the children.

"Yep," RJ said. "A few times."

"Figured so, big guy," James said. "Well, hope yous have fun in the Peach State. Oh, before we forget, kids." He stepped toward them, sliding his hands into his pockets again, his shoulders dropping as though he were about to make a confession of some sort. "At some point we want to give you two a—what's the word?"

"A keepsake," Ella offered.

"Yeah, a keepsake," he said without looking at Ella. "We want to give you two—all three of you—keepsakes from Morgan's room. One of his caps or sketches, or something." Many of Fervent's residents liked Morgan's drawings. Some of the women had asked him to sketch portraits of them. He did a few, but he knew his strengths and weaknesses when it came to drawing. Morgan liked to sit by the riverbank, which was only a seven- or eight-minute walk from their houses, and capture whatever caught his eye that day: a house finch, a hawk, or the ducklings trailing one another in the water. He drew lovely renderings of the Rhinecliff Bridge.

"You keeping his record collection?" RJ asked. He had borrowed Morgan's Kool & the Gang albums so much that, just last year, Morgan had given them to him. But when Syl had overheard RJ telling GiGi, she'd made him return the records to Morgan. She wasn't about to let her son bug people into giving him things.

"I'll go through them and see what we might want to keep," James said. "We'll let you come look through the rest. But that all might be months from now." To Syl, it sounded like an apology. "We need more time to be with his things."

"Well, we don't know any of the bands on those records," Ella said, surprising Syl. "Why don't you two come over the day before you leave town and get a few records each? Everything else will be off-limits for a while longer, though."

"Are you sure, Ella?" Syl asked. "They can wait till you—"

"He loved you all, Sylvia. The kids can definitely have some of his music now. No need to wait on that. I mean it. It's fine."

GiGi and RJ both thanked Ella.

"Speaking of his things," James said, "we gotta gather the strength to open the box the D.C. police gave to my mom."

"Box?" Syl asked.

James said that his mother had been given a box of Morgan's belongings when she'd gone to D.C. to identify his body. The elder Mrs. White had barely glanced inside. It held only the backpack he had traveled with. Inside were some snacks, a journal, his wallet, and a bunch of pencils. The few changes of clothes he'd taken had been left in his motel room, they assumed—though the motel staff never recovered anything.

A journal? Shit! Syl had to lean against the wall for support.

"Oh," she said, wondering if her heart would beat its way out of her chest. "I didn't know Morgan kept a journal."

"We started at the same time, about three years ago," GiGi said.

"I never read them, of course, but I think he mostly just jotted down notes," Ella said. "To-do lists, records and comic books to buy. That sort of thing. He sketched in journals, too."

Ella went on to say that her mother-in-law had taped the cardboard box shut and never opened it again. She had planned to bury it in a park somewhere in Queens, a park Morgan had enjoyed sitting in when he'd visited her for long weekends—which had been only a couple times a year.

"Mom just couldn't bring herself to bury it, though," James said. "Good thing she didn't, because here we are. Home."

"Only if you're sure, Miss Ella. About giving us the records, I mean," GiGi said, which made Syl feel proud. GiGi was becoming a mature young woman. And Syl believed her daughter was coming to resemble her more and more with each passing year: the russet-brown complexion, sharp nose, round face, long neck, and soft voice, all of which Syl had inherited from her own mother. For a long time, GiGi had looked like Reggie's mother and sisters. "Whenever you're ready, we'll be happy for whatever you let us have of his," GiGi said to the Whites. RJ nodded in agreement.

"Why don't you all come over about this time on Saturday?" Ella said. "That would give me two whole days to look through the records, just in case Morgan had some Beatles albums mixed in with the pop music he loved," she said. GiGi and RJ said that would work fine, since they would be heading out Sunday morning.

"I imagine that won't be easy," Syl said. "Opening the box. You sure you even *want* to?"

"No, but I think we *need* to," Ella said somberly. "It might be a month from now, or even a year. But we have to."

"No question about it," James concurred.

Syl didn't believe Morgan was the type to write out pages about his feelings or conversations he'd had. In the year she'd become like a close aunt to him, he'd kept their conversations fairly surface-level. The journal was probably full of drawings or simple things, like Amtrak departure times, motel phone numbers, and addresses. She steadied her breathing. *This is nothing to worry over, Syl,* she told herself. *He didn't write anything about the secret in his journal. No good can come of them knowing I'm the reason he went to D.C. and got on that city train.*

"Anyway, we're lookin' forward to settlin' back into our home and into our freedom. Get used to doing regular things again,"

James said. "Like fishin'. I want to go fishin' so bad I don't know what to do. Calms me, you know?"

Syl nodded, remembering that it was a pastime Morgan had tried but had no real interest in.

"It'll be a long time before I go to another drive-in movie," Ella said. "*If* I ever do."

"You can say that again," James said just before they waved goodbye to Gigi and RJ. Ella gave Syl another hug before they stepped, one by one, off the porch. They didn't turn back around as Syl watched them walk down the driveway.

Syl thought then how neither of them had mentioned Paul Hope, how sorry they felt for what happened to him, or any concern for his wife and daughters.

CHAPTER THREE

On January 9, 1981, nearly six months after Paul Hope was found dead, a jury had found James and Ella White guilty of his murder. On the July night Mr. Hope was killed, the Whites got into a fight with Paul and his wife, Reba, at the drive-in movie on Route 9. The hit film *Airplane!* had been released the previous week. It was all the rage.

One set of witnesses claimed to have seen James and Paul exchanging words near the concession stand. James was carrying a tray with two drinks and popcorn; Paul hadn't bought his and Reba's yet. Witnesses said James walked over to Paul and said, "I heard about what you said to my son when he said hello to your daughter. They're classmates, asshole. Only reason I haven't cracked your head open is because he and my wife begged me not to." It was said that Paul Hope then replied, "It would be best if you keep walking. I could have you in jail in thirty minutes, and you know it. Just keep walking, White." And James said, "I will, for now. I don't want all these people to see me knock your teeth out."

After the movie ended, both couples were throwing away their trash at the same time. Paul Hope said something under his breath but loud enough for James to hear.

Two awful, softly whispered words from one white man to another.

"What was the *something* you heard Mr. Hope say to Mr. White, ma'am?" a lanky police officer had asked an eyewitness at the drive-in. A staff member at the ticket booth had seen the fight and called the police.

"Is Mr. Hope the one with blond hair or the one with dark hair?" the woman asked.

"Hope is the blond one," the officer clarified, and he looked at the witness as though that was something she ought to know.

"I'm not from around here, just so you know," she said, dabbing sweat from her forehead and neck with a napkin. "Anyway, the blond one said—" She paused and looked off into the distance. "You want me to say it? The exact words?"

"Yes, I do. Please."

"Okay," she said. "But I'm only repeating it because you need to know why the brunette guy hauled off and hit the blond one."

"Just tell the man what you heard, Sherry," a man standing next to her urged. He looked exasperated.

"Nigger lover," she said. "That's what the blond guy said to the brunette man. That's what he called him. Then they started fighting like a couple of bulldogs or something. People tried breaking them up, but those two were really going at each other. And their wives were, *too.* Gosh, it was a wild thing to see, sir. All four of them had a bleeding lip, earlobe, or nose. It was just terrible." She went on to say that a group of men were finally able to pull both couples apart and escort them to their cars.

The Hopes drove off first, other witnesses reported. The Whites left a few minutes after them.

When later questioned by officers, James willingly admitted that he and Paul Hope had exchanged words and fought. There was no shame in that, James said on the record. He even admitted that he'd wanted to follow Mr. Hope and finish the fight. But

Ella wouldn't allow it. James's nose was bleeding heavily enough as it was, they'd told the police.

James and Ella swore in statements that they'd pulled over at Richmont's Petro. When asked by investigators why she had so much blood on her hands when she entered the store, she said her instinct had been to do whatever she could to stop her husband's bleeding. She had reached over to James's face, cradling it, not thinking.

Porter Venable, the pimply—though well beyond his pubescent years—grandson of the original owners of Richmont's, corroborated James and Ella's story. But he shared something the Whites hadn't.

"Mr. Venable," Irvin Orsay, the stout, slow moving, slow-speaking, white-haired prosecutor said during the trial. Syl wondered if Orsay would do better to sit down. He looked as though he might keel over at any moment. Syl also thought he sounded more like a Bostonian than a New Yorker.

Syl had been in the courtroom that day—not in support of the Whites, necessarily, but because she'd been curious to hear, firsthand, if the evidence against her neighbors was strong. She hadn't been entirely convinced. "Did you have an interaction with defendant Ella White on the evening of July 12, 1980?" Orsay asked.

"Yes, sir," Porter replied.

"Please describe that interaction."

"Well, she certainly wasn't her usual nice self," Porter said, combing his long red hair back with his fingers. "She said something pretty damn shocking."

"Go on."

"Well, I guess my questions were getting on her nerves. I mean, shit, do you blame me for being curious? There was blood *everywhere*."

"Mr. Venable, we can do without the profanity, thank you," Judge Berk, a dead ringer for Carol Burnett, interrupted. She nodded for the prosecutor to resume.

"What were some of your questions?"

"I asked her where all the blood came from and if she needed me to call an ambulance or something. She said, 'No police, no ambulances. Just napkins or paper towels. Now!' So I handed her the roll of paper towels we keep at the register. People are always spilling their coffee and stuff."

"What was the shocking thing she said to you, Mr. Venable?"

"I can't remember what my next question to her was, *exactly,* but her answer was 'If you ask one more *goddamn* question, I swear you'll get what Paul Hope has coming to him. *You'll* be the one bleeding out. Now hand me that *fucking* bottle of peroxide!' She threw a couple of dollars on the counter and left. The dollars had bloody fingerprints on them so I just used some napkins to scoop them into the waste bin."

Syl wasn't surprised to hear that Ella had behaved that way to Venable. She'd seen her snap at innocent people before. And though she'd never witnessed Ella being harsh with Morgan, and he'd denied ever being mistreated by Ella, Syl had always felt unsure.

"Just so we're clear here," Orsay said. "You heard Ella White say that Paul Hope had something coming to him that would cause him to bleed out. Is that correct?"

"Yes, sir."

The prosecutor turned to the jury. "I'd say that sounds pretty premeditated."

"Objection!" the Whites' attorney yelled from his seat, but the thought had set in, as it was intended to.

CHAPTER FOUR

Syl, with GiGi and RJ by her side, watched the Whites walk out of their yard and to the right, toward their own house, which was two nearly identical ranch-style houses away. All of the houses in Fervent looked similar: Boxy. Tract houses. Some of the houses had basements, but most didn't. Each owner painted their house a different color from the ones directly next door to them. Syl's was sky blue. And in the front, there were six evenly spaced shrubs that Fate trimmed for her during the summer months. Syl wasn't interested in yard décor. It simply never appealed to her.

Fate's house was canary yellow, and his colorful flower beds reminded Syl of the aerial views one might see while watching *Knots Landing*. Mrs. Talbot's white-brick house was surrounded by one continuous bed of white and yellow flowers. Syl didn't know the names of them.

The Whites' house was the color of natural clay. Much like Syl, they kept a yard mostly free of adornment. They did, however, have two leafy green bushes, one on each side of their front door.

Syl knew that at least one neighbor (usually Mrs. Talbot, if she didn't have guests at the time) was probably looking out their window, noting the time the Whites were leaving, which direction their hair was blowing, which one walked in front of the other.

"You're in the clear, Ma," RJ said. He dropped himself onto the couch and began kicking his sneakers off. "They don't seem mad at you about your trial testimony."

Neither of Syl's children knew the secret. If they did, and if they were to learn that Syl's telling of it led Morgan to D.C., where he got on the inner-city train, they would never forgive her, she feared.

"Put those shoes *right* back on, and get up," Syl ordered. "We're still going to Mrs. Talbot's to congratulate her."

"I don't see why we have to go," RJ said.

"Because she gives you two a 'Congratulations' card at the end of each school year. It won't kill y'all to go and return a little bit of cheer and have a piece of cake. And I don't know why you *still* think the Whites would be mad at me about my testimony? I only confirmed what the jury had already heard or read about my little injury. I don't understand why people were still talking about that."

Syl and James had had an incident at work that left her with eight stitches over her right eye. Aco, Inc., nearly pressed charges against him. But Syl begged them not to. It wasn't as though he'd thrown a toy *at* her face. The toy he threw at the wall ricocheted and hit her eyebrow.

"That's still snitching," GiGi said, refreshing her ponytail.

"Yep," RJ added. "You didn't like them."

"She still doesn't," GiGi added, making Syl wonder if it was that obvious.

"You never heard me say I didn't like James and Ella, Gi," Syl shot back. And it was true. Syl had never spoken those words to her children.

"But, Ma," GiGi said, "you used to always say they weren't feeding Morgan the kinds of foods Black kids need to try, and that they weren't getting him the right kinds of lotions for Black people's skin. Stuff like that."

Syl couldn't argue with those things, but it was the fact that Morgan wasn't allowed to watch sitcoms with Black families and the fact that he'd never visited a Black church that bothered Syl most. Did Syl think it was wonderful that Ella cared for her Black orphanage sister's baby? Yes. Did Syl think Ella and James were doing the best they could to make sure Morgan knew as much as possible about what it was like to be a Black person—a Black male—in the world? No.

Those irritations with the Whites didn't even include how they'd treated her gay best friend, Fate.

Syl and the children had talked about snitching many times. *Remember to plead the Fifth if the cops and lawyers try to make you rat people out,* the two of them had said during the trial. They'd watched too many reruns of *The Bold Ones.* It was a program their father loved. Syl also enjoyed detective and courtroom dramas, but she always preferred *Barnaby Jones* over the ones Reggie watched.

"I'm not doing this with you two again. I've never snitched 'bout anything in my life. And hush up about it before I get angry. Shit. Those two already messed up the rest of my day."

"See," GiGi said, teasing, "you don't like them."

Syl walked to the kitchen, out of her children's sight, where she dabbed the sweat from her forehead and neck with a sheet of ScotTowels. Her perspiration soaked the tacky artwork that was printed on the paper: a jar labeled *Milk,* one labeled *Sugar,* one labeled *Flour.*

She pulled the pitcher of cold water from the olive-green Frigidaire, poured herself a glass, and drank it straight down. It gave her some relief.

—

On the day Ella let the secret slip—it was in the winter of '75—she and James were in one of their rough patches. Syl, who had just parked and was about to run into the grocery store to grab a block of cheddar cheese and canned milk, saw Ella sitting in her ten-year-old Buick Electra. She was crying. With a gloved finger, Syl tapped on the window and Ella flinched, stared at her for a moment, then motioned for her to go around and get in on the passenger side. Syl got in, expecting relief from the icy temperatures, only to find that Ella didn't have the heat on.

There were a few balled-up fast-food napkins in her lap, a hairbrush on the dashboard, and an empty RC Cola bottle on the passenger-side floor. Still, it was much cleaner than the pickup truck James drove daily. Just passing his truck in Aco's parking lot, one could see receipts and napkins and cardboard burger holders piled all around. It wasn't a good example to set for Morgan, Syl thought.

That day, Ella told Syl that James had been bullying Morgan.

"Bullying?" Syl had asked. "Ella, is he safe with James?"

Syl remembered fantasizing about having some of her distant family members from down south come to whisk Morgan away and raise him—somewhere the Whites would never think to look.

"Of course, he's safe with me and James," Ella said with a frown, clearly annoyed by the question. "It's not *real* bullying, exactly," she said, picking at a piece of rough plastic on the steering wheel. "With Morgan being short for his age, James wants him to toughen up and be more intimidating. He *wants* the kid to have a Napoleon complex."

"Wow," Syl said, folding her arms over her chest. "And what do you say when James does this?"

Ella didn't like the question. She, too, folded her arms across her chest.

"I don't just sit there and let it happen, Sylvia, if that's what you're implying. But I have to allow those two to have a father-son relationship. They have to bond as two guys."

"I understand what you mean about them bonding, but I—"

"*Morgan* doesn't have issues with being short. He couldn't care less, Sylvia. His birth father's a short man. His birth mom isn't exactly a tall woman. When I saw them a couple of years ago in D.C., they—"

"Whoa, whoa. Wait a second," Syl said, turning her body on the cracked leather car seat to face Ella. "I thought Morgan's blood parents had died from overdosing."

Ella let her chin drop to her chest and placed both hands over her face. "Shit!" she shouted and pounded the steering wheel. "Shit, shit, shit!"

She looked out her side window. Then she said, "Well, I might as well tell you everything. Well, not everything. We'd be here all week."

Ella explained that she and Morgan's birth mother, Gwinette, were raised in the same Champaign, Illinois, orphanage. Ella was older by nine years. By the time eleven-year-old Gwinette was entering the orphanage, Ella had come of age but was still living there, working in exchange for room and board. But the two had become close in the two years they overlapped. To Ella, she was like a little sister.

"Oh, Sylvia, she was probably the brightest kid to come through there in many years. I was in charge of getting the new girls acclimated with routines and that sort of thing. One day, Gwin came to my doorway and said, 'Ella, I've decided I'm not Catholic. Does that mean I can leave now?' I asked her where she'd go, and she looked me in my eyes and said, 'I don't know, but I'm getting the hell outta here.'" Syl and Ella both giggled. "I told her she couldn't curse and she said hell was a place, not a curse. She was full of cute comebacks, Sylvia. But she was an unsettled child. Smart, but had trouble focusing for long periods of time. Morgan is like that, you know." Syl had noticed. "Anyway, I liked her strength and how even though she'd been abandoned, she didn't seem to let that dictate how she thought about herself. At eleven years old she knew what she wanted, which was to get the hell out of the Catholic orphanage."

Syl sat silently, taking in Ella's story and the pride and sadness with which she told it.

"I had a younger sister who was around eleven or twelve," Ella said. "Never met her, of course, but I learned of her through nuns who got information from this one and that one. And, I don't know, I guess I imagined my little sister was sharp and headstrong, too. Even though my half sister was white, and my new orphanage sister, so to speak, was Black, I felt a kinship," Ella added with a shrug.

Ella went on to tell Syl that she and Gwinette baked cookies together, when permitted. They brushed and braided each other's hair and played marbles. And once in a while, they cried together because they didn't know where their family members were or if they'd ever see them again.

"Gwin was the only Black girl there for about five or six months. The girls around my age asked why I gave her so much attention. I said to them, 'I could ask you why *you're* not giving her *any* attention.' We all knew the answer, just like you and I know the answer right now, Sylvia."

"Yes, I do," Syl said.

"Anyway, I told those girls I'd put snakes in their beds if they didn't leave Gwin alone. She and I were a little team. I know now that it's not so good to use one person to replace another, but I didn't know that's what was happening, and I still care for Gwinette just like she's my little sister—the one I don't know."

"I understand," Syl assured her.

So when Gwinette contacted Ella in '61 and told her that she and her boyfriend were about to have a baby they couldn't keep, Ella said that she and James would adopt it. At the time, Ella and Gwinette had been speaking once every few months. Gwinette knew Ella wanted a baby with James and that they hadn't been able to have one, though the doctors were stumped as to why.

"He was a gift, wasn't he?" Syl asked.

"Yes, he was," Ella mused, smiling and dabbing at her tears. "Gwinette and I gave each other gifts. She gave me Morgan, and I gave her the time she still needed to grow up."

"It was very kind of you. But didn't his mother have anyone else she could ask to take her baby?"

"By anyone else, you mean a Black family. Don't you?" Ella didn't give Syl a chance to answer, but she had guessed right. "Sylvia, this is hurtful. You've questioned my mothering of Morgan before. I don't know why I just told— Shit! Shit! Shit!"

"Ella."

Then, in a panic, Ella said, "Sylvia, you're not going to tell anyone about this, are you? You won't tell Morgan, will you?" She reached over and grabbed Syl's hands and squeezed them. "Listen, I know your true feelings, and I know we're not exactly friends. But you'd destroy the stability I've given Morgan if you tell him or anyone else."

"Why not just tell him his parents were young and not ready?"

"*Swear* to me," Ella said. It was as though she hadn't heard the question. "Swear to me *now. Please.* Swear you'll take this secret to your grave. Knowing they're alive, and possibly meeting them, Sylvia, he'll wish he never did. Trust me. They aren't terrible people. They're just not equipped for parenthood. *Still.*"

Syl thought for a few moments. *One day I'll wish I never heard this secret.*

"I do," Syl said. "I swear. I'd never do anything to hurt a child who's happy and safe. Just be the best mother you can be to him, Ella."

"I thought I was doing just that," Ella said.

Syl and Ella never spoke of it again.

After that conversation, Syl knew she would have to keep an even closer watch on Morgan.

CHAPTER FIVE

GiGi and RJ were still stuck on the topic of snitching when Syl walked back into the living room.

"The way Uncle Fate testified, that was all-out snitching," RJ said.

"Yep," GiGi said, the *p* sharp and certain. GiGi, Syl thought, had much of her father's personality: to the point about everything.

"Go on over to Mrs. Talbot's," Syl said, eager to call Fate and tell him about the Whites' visit. One of the kids sucked their teeth. "Now, please. Tell her I'll be there in a bit. I just need to do a couple of things so dinner'll be ready to eat when we get back."

The meatloaf was practically done, but she would leave the oven on at two hundred degrees to cook away whatever pink might be hiding in the middle. The kids couldn't stand any sign that their meat had once been a living thing.

Syl dialed Fate's number. He picked up after three rings.

"Did you see who just left my house?"

"I was drifting into a nap," he said. "Who?" And when she told him James and Ella had just visited, he said, "Say *what*?" His second-tenor voice was smooth, with a hint of panic.

"I know. I—"

"Did you let them in?"

"Not right away, but yeah," she said. "I still can't believe they moved back to Fervent, let alone stopped here at my house."

"Sylvia Leigh Upshaw!" he shouted. Syl and Fate were the same age—forty-one—but Syl had always believed he had a much older soul. Using her full name when he was in disagreement with her was straight out of some great-grandmother's handbook. "Are you crazy? I wouldn't have even gone to the door. What did they want? Do they know we told Morgan?"

"Doesn't seem like it. They were pretty nice, which was strange. They would've said something about it if they knew."

"Hmmm," Fate hummed. He asked Syl if her children were there for the Whites' visit and she told him they were. She shared with Fate how grateful they claimed to be about her and Fate having been so kind to Morgan while they were in prison.

"You know I don't trust those two, Fate. But I have to say, the thanks seemed real. From both of them. I don't think Morgan told them or anyone else about the secret."

There was a brief silence. She could hear him moving around on his bed.

"I guess you're right," he said. "James wouldn't have been able to not mention something that serious. Ella, either. They probably don't know. Gosh, why in the hell are they back in Fervent, Lord Jesus? I mean, I still say it's a shame they were ever convicted at all. You know James and Ella have no fan in me, but that evidence was so damned circumstantial, a pair of squirrels could have killed Paul Hope."

"We both know how it happened."

"Yes. American *justice*. But we've talked that subject into the ground and back up again."

Fate still had his suspicions about what had caused the argument and fight between the Whites and the Hopes at the drive-in the night Paul Hope was killed. Fate believed there was much more to it than a nasty epithet being hurled, leading to a brawl. But no one pressed: Paul Hope didn't like Black people, and he didn't like *white* people who *liked* Black people. It was as simple as that.

"Either way, I feel pretty sure they don't know what I told Morgan. I think he took it to the grave. May God rest his soul." Syl decided not to mention the box with Morgan's backpack just yet. The chances of him having written anything about the secret in his journal were slim to none. There was no need in getting Fate more worked up.

"May he rest peacefully," Fate said.

"I did what we thought was right," Syl reminded him.

Before Syl and Fate had sat Morgan down—a few days before his death—they had decided that Fate would be there only to console Morgan, if necessary. But after Syl broke the news, and Morgan just sat there silently, Fate said, "Would you ever consider looking for them?" Morgan shrugged and stared straight ahead at his television, which he'd turned all the way down. "To be absolutely clear," Fate added, "that's not what we're suggesting. In fact, I don't know that I would, honestly. I'm just asking. Syl and I just thought you have the right to know, in *case* you decide to seek them out—especially with James and Ella being unavailable to you now."

After Morgan was killed on the train, there were moments when Syl wished she hadn't told him what Ella and James had kept from him. But those moments were rare. He needed to know, she believed.

"Did they say anything about my testimony?" Fate asked her. "Jesus, they must hate me. Hate me *more,* I should say." Fate was getting nervous. Syl could hear the tremble in his voice, despite his trying to conceal it. She knew she had to lie.

"No, we only talked about Morgan, Mr. Talbot, things like that."

"Good, because do you remember what James said he'd do to me just a few years ago? He was *beyond* belligerent. They *both* were. I have the right to talk about it when someone asks. Hell, it happened to *me*."

Fate was right. He had a right to speak about the experience, even if the Whites had apologized many times. Ella had even gone to Fate a couple of days after the incident, asking for forgiveness.

Syl had told Fate over and over again that what he had said on the witness stand did not send the Whites to prison. There was plenty stacked against them before any of Fervent's residents were called to testify. Still, Fate talked himself in a circle until he felt at ease again.

"Anyway, they're back and they're grieving. As a mother, I can't help but want to forgive them for all the not-so-nice things they said and did in the past. And for not being the best parents I think they could've been to a Black child."

"I know. I feel for them. Losing a child while you're in prison"—he grunted—"and in prison for things you didn't *do*? Awful."

"It's just terrible. I—"

"But they aren't angels," Fate said.

"No, but they *are* two people who've been to hell and back, whether we like them or not."

"No shit." They both sighed. "Why on God's miserable earth would they want to live in Saugerties and Fervent, Syl? After everything that's happened, you'd think they'd sell the house, stay down in the city, or go to Ella's people in Illinois?"

"You know Ella doesn't have any people."

"I'm talking about that nun who pretty much raised her at the orphanage, and the girls she grew up with. I know she doesn't have *family* family. Don't you think that would've been better for them? A new life someplace else?"

"They said this is their home and they're not moving, Fate. I guess I understand that. Some."

"Do they think they're getting their old jobs back or something? I may have to get myself a new one if they let Ella come back to the high school."

Fate taught social studies at River Hudson High. He had been there for five years by the time Syl met him. Ella had worked at RHH as a secretary for both the main office and the nurse's office.

"You will *not* quit that job, Fate. You love RHH." Fate was one of the first three Black teachers hired at RHH, and he was very proud of that accomplishment. Secretly, Syl wondered if maybe she should consider looking for a new job. Yes, James had just shown her a calm and forgiving demeanor. But Fate was right: those two had sides, and James's anger could resurface once he returned to his old routines.

"You're damn right, I'm not quitting my job. Principal Sorkin *loves* me. Did I tell you he and I both attended Bard College?" Syl nodded. "And Syl, I adore my students and the work I do. You think the school will let her come back? The brawl *alone.*" He shook his head. "There's no way the factory would let James back in there, would they?"

"Well, maybe the Whites don't want those jobs back," Syl offered with hope. "But I don't know how the laws work. They might be entitled to them."

"I doubt that. No one's entitled to shit here."

"Yeah, well, James and Ella are innocent of murder. And

they're white. Either way, they want a fresh start, and they deserve one." Syl meant that sincerely. "Let's be neighborly. We don't have to be their friends, though."

"I never thought they'd get out of those prisons, Syl. Never."

"Me, neither." Syl remembered wondering, just a few weeks after the Whites had been sentenced, how long it took an inmate to get used to being in prison—or if they ever really got used to it at all. "I should've written to them at least once. Ella will hold that against me and blurt it out one day."

"Probably," Fate said. Then, without taking a beat: "They would've definitely said something if they knew what we told Morgan, right?"

Damn it! Syl thought. She knew she wouldn't be able to keep it from Fate that a journal existed. He'd be worried to death.

"Listen to me, and listen to me good before you panic."

"Oh shit. I *knew* you weren't telling me everything. I *felt* it!"

Syl told Fate about the box of Morgan's belongings that had been returned to the elder Mrs. White by the D.C. authorities, and that there was a journal.

"A journal? Morgan kept a journal?"

"Yeah, I didn't know until they just mentioned it."

"Well, do you think he'd write about us in it?" Fate asked. "He wasn't that type. Was he?"

"Exactly. I doubt it. But—"

"Where is this box with this journal?" Fate asked, and Syl told him that James and Ella now had it.

"Why?" she asked. "What are you going to do? Break in and look for it?"

"Don't tempt me. Shouldn't be hard to find. A taped-up box with police markings and labels all over it, probably."

"Fate!" Syl exclaimed. "Don't be crazy."

"I'm not being serious. I'm not going to jail for a journal."

Syl and Fate were quiet for a few seconds.

"Goddamn it, Syl. Fuck! They will burn our houses down with us in them if they find out what we told Morgan."

"I know!" Syl said.

"But hold on. Let's be sensible. Morgan wouldn't write about the secret. He wouldn't."

"I really don't think so, Fate. I just don't."

"Okay, let's drop it for now, before we get carried away."

"I agree," Syl said. "They said it might be a year before they even open that box. I hope they never do." She told Fate that she and the kids would be going over to look through albums.

"Maybe we should burn *their* house down when they're out."

"Fate!"

"Girl, I didn't mean it. Let's drop it." Syl knew he wouldn't drop it for long. If she was nervous about the journal, Fate was definitely worried about it. "Well, when you go over there with the kids to look through the music, see if—"

"I'm not breaking a box open, Fate."

"Hmmm," he hummed.

"When are you going to Mrs. Talbot's party?"

"I called her. I'll go have a piece of the cake tomorrow when I take her a little congrats gift. I'm not in the mood today. I told her my knee's bothering me again. I'm also not up for all the talk about the Whites being back."

"Making me go it alone, huh?" Syl said. "Let's not worry about this journal business, Fate. Okay?"

"Have you forgotten who you're talking to? I'm going to worry about that journal for at least the next couple of days. But seriously, I don't think the boy wrote anything serious in it."

CHAPTER SIX

Fate was the best friend Syl had ever had. The pair met in '73, one week after the Upshaws moved to Fervent from the Bronx. Syl got the job at the toy factory, and she and Reggie agreed that relocating upstate made sense.

Reggie was working as a full-time building superintendent, overseeing the maintenance for three different properties in the Bronx, so he stayed in the city for a few months after Syl and the children moved to Fervent. Reggie came up to Saugerties on weekends and eventually got full-time facilities work at a nearby college.

Fate introduced himself to Syl on a Saturday afternoon. She was alone that day. GiGi and RJ were down in the Bronx with Reggie, attending a birthday party. Syl had done a big haul at the grocery store—her back seat was full, and she had another five or six bags in the trunk, which Fate must have seen from his window.

"Hey!" he shouted, approaching her driveway, and her royal blue '71 Chevelle, on foot. To Syl, he looked very much like Wilson Pickett. "Hold on. I'll help you."

Fate was wearing a corn-yellow-and-blue plaid long-sleeve button-up shirt and a pair of slacks that perfectly matched the shirt's blue. He sported an Afro Syl estimated to be at least five inches out from his scalp. He smelled of Jōvan Musk. She had wanted to buy Reggie a bottle of it but knew he would use it only once or twice before forgetting all about it.

"Oh, I'm fine," Syl said. "It's only a few bags."

"I've seen you take a *few* from the back seat already, and I see *more* than a few in your trunk. I'm Lafayette Jolly the Third. But I go by Fate." She could hear the North and the South battling in his accent. The North was winning.

"Nice meeting you, Fate. I'm Sylvia." She extended her hand and he took it. "Sylvia—"

"Upshaw. Your husband is Reginald, your daughter is Regina, nicknamed GiGi, and your son is Reginald Jr., but you all call him RJ." He also knew that Syl and Reggie were originally from the South and that the children were both born in the Bronx.

"Oh," she said. She liked this knowing of his. It reminded her of back home.

"It's my business to know these things, Sylvia. And it's Mrs. Talbot's business to make sure we *all* know these things."

"Is that right?" Syl asked with a smile, though she'd already figured out that Mrs. Talbot was the unofficial *Fervent Times.*

With two arms full of brown paper bags, Fate said, "Having her as a neighbor is a blessing and a curse. She tells everyone's business except her own, and *Mr.* Talbot instructs everyone on how they should cut their lawn, *water* their lawn, wash their car, *dry* their car. Two sweet old white people, though. Both of them. He's her third husband, you know."

"Her *third*? Get outta here." Syl was genuinely surprised. She had imagined they'd been together forty years or longer.

"See what I mean? She didn't mention that when she brought over that store-bought banana bread, did she?" He raised his eyebrows. "Now, unless you invite me in, I'll just set these bags on your porch, which I think would defeat the purpose of helping you."

Having invited Fate in, she said, "So, where are you from, Fate? I hear something in your accent."

"St. Louis. But my momma and daddy were from Mississippi. So I know my accent is all over the place."

In the kitchen, he set the bags on the counter, turned to Syl, and said, "Now, Sylvia, let's get something out of the way."

"Lay it on me," she replied, having a feeling she already knew what he was about to confide. But it was also possible he was about to give her a whole different set of neighborhood rules to follow.

"Well, first of all, that is a very nice color on you," he said. Syl was wearing a thin mint-green sweater and a pair of denims. She didn't care much about fashion, but she knew when two things matched or didn't.

Syl thanked him and said, "And you look as though you're about to model for the Sears catalog."

"You flatter me," he said. Then, with a straight face, he said, "Syl, I don't have a wife or a girlfriend."

"Okay."

"I haven't had a girlfriend since I was, I don't know, seventeen, eighteen years old."

"I'm listening." She had been right. Fate was gay—a fact Mrs. Talbot had already divulged—but Syl didn't want to interrupt him. He might tell her something she hadn't yet heard.

"But I have a very good friend named Vincent who lives in Manhattan, and we've been very, *very* close for the past six years. Seven years in December. We met at a Christmas party. Danced together a couple of times and have been *friends* ever since."

"Yeah? That sounds groovy," Syl said.

"It was, indeed," Fate said. "Vince hasn't had a girlfriend in many years, either. Do you follow me, Sylvia?"

"Yep."

"Good. Now, if any of that's a problem for you, after today simply avoid me, *aggressively*. Deal?"

"I'm not like that, Fate."

"What about your husband?"

"My husband is taken."

"By you, I hope."

Syl laughed harder than she'd intended. Fate winked and smiled.

"Now, tell me honestly: Will he have an issue with me?" Fate asked again. His smile had vanished. Syl understood this was an important question. No one wants to be harassed or otherwise mistreated in their own neighborhood.

"Don't worry about him. I mean that." She looked into the bag she was still holding against her chest. "Want some coffee and butter cookies?"

Fate paused, looking at her before answering. "You're going to make me abandon my diet, Sylvia."

"Call me *Syl*." Then, with trepidation, she asked, "You always speak this proper?"

"Yes, I do," he said. "Well, most of the time. But make no mistake: I'm still country as hell." He winked again.

They became fast friends. In the weeks that followed, Fate told Syl more about himself, his work, how he came to live in Fervent, about Vincent—his true love, he called him—and the many things that helped him get through life as a Southern-born-and-raised gay Black man living in rural New York.

"Sometimes I go sit in those woods for peace and quiet," he told her one day, a few months into their friendship, when she asked if he thought more houses would be built in Fervent. "I might sell and move if they clear those trees."

"Would you, really?"

"I sure would," he said. "I didn't move up here to have a thousand close neighbors. I moved up here for the peace. Well, I was offered the job first, then I realized I'd love the peace. Living in the city was a lot of fun, and you know I enjoy popping down there for a long day or for a couple nights. But it's a rat race and it was wearing me down, aging me too soon, believe it or not. I do miss being able to go to the Village anytime I want, though. Just a little."

Syl imagined that Saugerties having no gay bars was difficult for him, but everyone has to make sacrifices, she believed. She hoped their friendship offered him comfort.

Fate wasn't Reggie's favorite neighbor, but he tolerated Syl's friendship with him. Syl didn't give him a choice. "Just tell him not to talk about his *personal* business round my kids, Syl," Reggie had once said to her. Syl paid Reggie no mind. She and Fate had quickly become a formidable duo, and no one would get in the way of that.

Over the years Syl told Fate many private things about herself, her unhappy marriage, the minor problems she was having with the kids.

"RJ behaves well for his teachers, but they say he won't pay attention," she confided in him a couple of weeks into their friendship. They were in Fate's living room having some foreign beer he'd tried while down in the city; he'd brought a six-pack back with him. An episode of *Maude* was on the television. Fate loved any show Esther Rolle was in.

"You aren't paying me any mind, are you, Fate?"

"I'm listening, but you know my show is on." Syl stopped talking and waited for a commercial.

"One of his teachers suggested we ask his pediatrician about something called Ritalin."

"Oh, yes. I know of a few students who take it. Listen: it helps. Y'all talk to the doctor. Problems with attention span are very common in boys, so y'all's insurance will probably take care of it. I'm fixin' to give half my students something to chill them out."

"Two *y'alls* and a *fixin'* in one day? You missing home or something?" Syl teased.

"I keep telling you I'm country," Fate said, crossing one leg over the other. "Does GiGi have any learning or attention span troubles?"

"No," Syl replied. "She's fine in that department. Our trouble with her is that she wants blond hair and blue eyes. But I guess with who they see all the time on TV, many Black kids want that."

"Yeah, well, that will fix itself over time."

"Then there's Reggie."

"Uh-oh," Fate said. "Please tell me he's faithful."

"As far as I know, he is. But I see him looking at women who don't look *anything* like me."

"White women?" Fate said.

"Not really," Syl said. Fate raised his eyebrows. "I see him looking at women with more meat on their bones than me."

"Interesting," he mused. "Has he asked you to gain weight?"

"Not directly, but when we—you know."

"Make love?"

"Yes. He tries to make things jiggle that just don't jiggle. So I know he wishes I had more to grab on to. I've tried, but I'm just built like my mother and aunts. I may not start to hold weight until I'm sixty."

"He might just be temporarily desiring something different,"

Fate offered. "It doesn't mean he'll leave you for a bigger woman. I see other men from time to time—just for a roll in the hay, though. Nothing serious."

"Fate!"

"What? It's only because they look different from Vincent. Not better, just different. But I'd never *leave* Vince for a man with a big chest and biceps."

"So you think it's fine if Reggie has a fling with a woman if it's just sex?"

"That's not quite what I'm saying. But, Syl, don't you see good-looking men all the time who don't look anything like Reggie?"

"Yes, but—"

"But *nothing.* It's human. Now, if he has an *affair,* you have a problem. *You* two are married and have a family. My situation is a little different. Syl, you're making me miss my show, but I'll give you this short lesson, if I may."

"Go ahead," Syl said. Fate sat his beer bottle down on a Niagara Falls coaster and leaned forward in his chair.

"I know a lot of gay men who want to live what I consider to be *straight people's* lives. One is kind of the husband, the other is the wife. They're very *traditional,* I guess you can say." He got up and turned the television's volume all the way down, then took his seat again. "But many of us have accepted that we're *not* straight people, and we don't pretend our relationships are like a straight couple's. We know and *love* that just because we have a main person, it doesn't mean we can't explore."

"Got it," Syl said. "Does Vince know you're seeing other men from time to time?"

"I'm sure he assumes I do, but he hasn't asked, nor do I ask him." Fate leaned back in his chair and picked the beer bottle back up. "Why? You think he should know, flat out?"

"I ain't getting in y'all's business," Syl said, then giggled.

"An *ain't* and a *y'all* in one sentence," Fate said. "Must be something in this beer." They clinked their bottles together. "He's probably sleeping with guys down in the city. Neither of us has ever had VD. We're smart men, so—" He didn't finish the sentence. He got back up to raise the television's volume, and they watched the rest of the *Maude* episode.

Syl and Fate had conversations like that all the time, over months and then years, and not a single time did any of what she shared with Fate come back to her from the lips of anyone else. So she told Fate the secret Ella had told her about Morgan's birth parents.

"His blood relatives could be terrible people," Fate said when Syl proposed the idea of telling Morgan. They were down at the riverbank, sitting on a bench Mr. Talbot had built. It was cold outside, but there was no wind.

"But they could be wonderful people. What if they're now a stable couple with good jobs and all? And they're Black, Fate. That's what he's needed all along, if you ask me."

"I'll say what I've always said on that whole Black child, white parents topic," Fate said, then inhaled deeply. "Yes, Black kids probably do get a better understanding of what it is to be Black when the people raising them are also Black. But—"

"I know what you're going to say. A safe home with parents who look different is better than no home or living with people who look like you but mistreat you. And I hear you, but—"

"Then let's leave that alone so we don't fall out," Fate said.

"Anyway, to Morgan, James and Ella may as well be dead."

"True, but I need to think about this, Syl."

"I don't see why you don't think it's right to do. I should've told him a long time ago—when I started to see they weren't nice people."

"No, the hell you shouldn't have, Syl. Shit."

Syl sighed and scratched her scalp with one finger. There was no itch.

"They're the only parents he knows, regardless of what he or we think of them. Don't tell him just now," Fate recommended. "Mull it over for a bit."

Syl took Fate's advice, and a couple of weeks later, just as she was about to ask him if he would go along with her to have the talk with Morgan, he called and said, "Syl, I think it's only right that Morgan *knows* about his other set of parents. He deserves the opportunity to do what he will with that information."

On Sunday, January 10, of this year, Syl and Fate took Morgan plates of baked chicken, vegetables, spaghetti, and homemade cake. Syl told him she had something important to tell him. He asked only one question after she shared the secret: "Did Ella ever say where they might be?"

"All I remember her saying was D.C., and that you were named Morgan because it's your birth father's last name."

She stared at him, wondering how he felt. Morgan could be hard to read, but there was something optimistic in the slight upturn at the corners of his lips and the faint rise of his eyebrows. He was wearing the forest-green sweat suit Syl, GiGi, and RJ had gotten him for Christmas. She had worried he might hate the color, but her kids told her he'd wear cotton-candy pink if they got it for him. He didn't care.

"Morgan John Morgan," he said with a chuckle. "I like the sound of my new name already." Syl and Fate exchanged glances while Morgan scratched his cornrows gently. GiGi had just done them for him the day before, and she'd put tiny blue rubber bands at the ends so they wouldn't unravel too quickly. "Maybe I'd like to find them. I don't know."

"That's your decision to make, fella," Syl said. "I just thought you had the right to *know*, since the Whites are—"

"Murderers," Morgan said. "And liars, too, evidently."

"Well—" She stopped short, because what could she say?

Syl asked Morgan if he would mind keeping what she'd just told him to himself.

"Your mom swore me to secrecy, but—"

"Ella," he corrected her.

"And if you decide to share it with my two, I just ask that you not tell them I was the one who told you. Please, Morgan."

"I don't think I'll talk to anyone about it, Aunt Syl," he said. "Not even Ella and James." Syl felt relief. GiGi would've told her she should've minded her own business, and she would have been right. Just before Syl and Fate were leaving Morgan's house, Morgan said, "Aunt Syl."

"Yeah, sweetheart."

"Gi and RJ are lucky to have you and Reggie—even though you two aren't together anymore." Syl teared up instantly, and Fate rubbed her shoulder. "Don't get me wrong; Ella and James love me a lot, and I love them, too. But I'd be lying if I said I didn't wish I was your son. The fact that you didn't tell me this years ago shows you put me ahead of what you were thinking about my parents, or whatever they are. You didn't wanna disturb my life. I appreciate that, Aunt Syl."

"Oh, baby," Syl said, and she threw her arms around Morgan. Fate joined the hug.

"You'd be a good father, too, Fate."

"A *good* father? Are you kidding?" Fate said. "I'd be a *wonderful* father. But no thanks."

Syl and Morgan smiled at each other.

On the following Tuesday, one of the women who worked in

the main office at the factory made an announcement on the intercom, asking Syl to come upstairs. She said there was an emergency phone call. It was Morgan.

"Aunt Syl," he said, "I'm going to see if I can find them. Well, him at least. Mr. Morgan."

"You sure about this, honey? All you have is a last name. Shouldn't you take some time to think it over?"

"I want to do it now, while I feel interested. I may start scrolling through all the Morgans in the phone book and change my mind soon after. But I at least want to get started on that long list. Do you remember if Ella told you my real mom's name?"

Syl could only remember that it ended in *ette,* and she shared that bit of information with Morgan.

"Jean*ette,* Lyn*ette,* I won't for*get,*" he joked.

If Syl weren't so worried that he'd be disappointed, she might have laughed.

Morgan said that he had asked a co-worker to cover his shifts. Even before he'd graduated from high school he'd worked at the Kmart on Route 9, headed toward Kingston. They gave him almost full-time hours, and after the Whites went to prison, Morgan kept the mortgage and other bills paid, since the property hadn't been seized.

"James's mom wants me to sell it and move away from Fervent," he had told Syl shortly after James and Ella went to prison. "But *I* didn't kill anyone and *I* don't need to run away. I'm staying right here in my home, Aunt Syl. Until I get tired of it." He'd vowed to do whatever was necessary to keep it, and he had.

"Where will you stay in D.C., sweetie? Is there a friend who can go along with you?" She'd known the answer before she asked. Morgan had always been mostly a loner. He only ever allowed GiGi and RJ to take up a few hours of his time per week.

He gave his co-workers about the same amount of time outside of work.

Morgan told Syl not to worry. He would be alright, he said.

"I promise to call at least once while I'm away, Aunt Syl." And he did. He called when he got to his motel room later that evening to tell her he had arrived in D.C.

"I'm glad you got there safely. Be sure to get a hot meal and some good sleep," Syl said. "How will you get around there in D.C. to do your searching? Taxi fare will add up quickly."

"They have buses and trains here, Aunt Syl," he said. "Just like in New York City." He chuckled.

"I'm being silly, aren't I? Please be careful and call me in a couple days. Give me the number to that motel, please." She jotted it down on the back of a grocery store receipt.

But Fate told Syl that she shouldn't expect Morgan to keep calling.

"Forget it. A young man on that kind of mission isn't calling his neighbors to check in."

That Friday, the news broke about the Metro derailment. The reporters kept referring to it as "the Orange Line." Syl knew nothing about D.C.'s public transportation system and set the whole disaster aside in her mind. But on that Sunday afternoon, the names of the people who'd been killed in the derailment were released. She told her kids that Morgan had gone to visit someone in the D.C. area and that someone by the name of Morgan White had died in that crash.

For hours, Syl called Morgan's motel. The phone in his room rang and rang. No answer. Syl knew her children hadn't watched the news, and she doubted their friends did either. She called Fate and asked him to come over.

"Fate, if Morgan was on that train, I—" A clipped wail escaped her and she collapsed into her best friend's arms just inside her front door. After a few minutes of sobbing, he escorted her to the nearest chair.

"We have to wait and see," he said, rubbing her back.

"I told the front desk to tell him there was an emergency and to please call back," Syl said, gasping between words. "Lord, please make him call."

"What have we done?" Fate whispered, shaking his head. "What have we done?"

A full day passed and Morgan hadn't called.

"That doesn't mean it was *our* Morgan, though," GiGi said. She was standing at the bathroom sink, in the middle of hot-combing her hair. Syl worried that her daughter might punch her for even having suggested it was their Morgan. GiGi threw the comb into the basin, went to her room, and screamed. Her shouts bounced from wall to wall. Syl, RJ, and Fate sat in the living room, wiping their tears and noses with toilet tissue. They had used all the Kleenex.

They held each other's hands, cried, and moaned.

When RJ went out for a walk, Syl said to Fate, "We have to call his grandmother. I doubt he told her he was going on a trip, but still, if it's him, she has to be told—someone in his family has to know."

Mrs. Carrie White thought it was foolish of Syl and Fate to assume that the man who shared a name with her grandson was her grandson.

"Come on, Sylvia," she scolded in her very distinct Queens accent. "There's probably a thousand Morgan Whites just right here in Corona. Imagine how many there are in this country. You stop that crying. Really, now. Let's be sensible, dear. Why would Morgan be in D.C.? We don't have family there. Ella certainly doesn't."

"He said he needed a trip and wanted to go sightseeing, ma'am."

"Sightseeing this time of year?"

"That's what he said, Mrs. White." Syl sobbed. The crying had nothing to do with the acute guilt she felt over telling Mrs. White a lie. The thought of having possibly lost such a smart, kind person who'd become like family—it was ripping her heart to shreds.

"Well, I guess he's an adult and can sightsee whenever he wants. But Morgan *hates* winter." That wasn't true. He loved winter, but hated snow. "I wish he'd let me know he was going. Why do *you* know he went and didn't tell me sooner? You're not his family, Sylvia. When will you accept that?"

To that, Syl said nothing. She could have said a lot.

"Mrs. White," Syl said after catching her breath. "Do you think maybe you should call the D.C. police and see what they'll tell you? Maybe you can ask if they have a driver's license or something. If I call, they won't tell me anything."

"It's not your place to call and ask any questions in the first place. And I will do no such thing," she retorted. "Morgan will have his vacation and he'll be back up there in Saugerties next week, just as he said he would. If he calls you, tell him I'd very much like to speak to him. Thank you, and goodbye."

A couple of days later, Syl called Mrs. White again, this time to tell her that the manager at Morgan's motel said the young man hadn't returned to his room since the news broke of the train derailment. At that point, Mrs. White had no choice but to call the D.C. authorities. And when she called Syl back, about an hour later, she could barely get a word out.

"Morgan's no longer with us, Sylvia."

"My God," Syl said. Her legs trembled, and she lowered herself to the cold floor. She had been holding on to a thread of hope that Mrs. White's words had just snipped. Morgan, with his big heart, his innate sense of responsibility, and his comforting old soul, was really gone. Syl and Mrs. White sobbed into their phones until one of them hung up. Syl couldn't remember which one of them did so first.

A week later, Morgan was buried in Saugerties. He was not a religious person, so there was only a graveside service. Almost every family in Fervent was there, as were many of Morgan's former teachers and his co-workers.

For weeks after Morgan's passing, Syl was angry at the world. Angry with herself for telling him the secret. Mad at Ella and James for not having told him years ago. Furious at herself for not having told him sooner. Ticked off with anyone she knew who'd ever been anything but loving toward Morgan. Even driving past the Hopes' estate pissed her off.

"One thing that makes me feel a little better is that James at least got to land some good blows on Paul Hope for saying that awful thing about Morgan," Syl said to Fate. "Whether James and Ella really killed that man or not, I guess we'll never know."

"Who can say, Syl?" Fate replied. "Maybe they did."

CHAPTER SEVEN

When the Whites' trial began, Syl and Fate decided they wanted to be present for Reba Hope's testimony. They stood in the courthouse hallway, waiting to be let in. Syl wondered why it seemed all courthouses looked alike, no matter where they were: wood paneling, heavy wooden doors with dull gold doorknobs, linoleum that never looked clean, no matter how much it was mopped. And the place smelled as though someone had taken just one puff of a cigar and put it out.

"I feel nervous," Syl said to Fate.

"Me, too, but I don't know why."

"They're going to ask her about her husband's—" She searched her mind for the word. "His *appearance* when she found him. And we already know it wasn't a pretty sight."

Reba Hope was dressed in a black skirt suit with a matching black blouse.

"Good Lord," Fate whispered to Syl, his breath smelling of the two squares of spearmint gum he'd recently tossed into his mouth like Tylenol. "They're going *widow* all the way, I see."

"Well, she *is* a widow. Cool it."

When Reba took the stand, she testified that she and her husband drove straight home after the fight with the Whites. The Hopes didn't live in Fervent. Their large, beautiful log mansion was about a mile away, on the border between Saugerties and Woodstock. Shortly after Hope was murdered, while the Whites were in jail awaiting their trail, Mrs. Hope and their daughters had moved closer to New York City—Tarrytown, Syl had heard. It was also rumored that their house in Saugerties still hadn't been put up for sale.

Once they arrived at their house, they washed the drying blood from their swelling lips, noses, and knuckles before holding ice and other frozen things against those same aching areas, Reba said. From the kitchen sink, she saw two sets of headlights flickering up their long driveway. Paul grabbed his pistol and headed for the front yard, thinking it might be the Whites coming with backup. But it was friends of the Hopes', two couples, who had seen the fight and wanted to check on them.

"Who were the two couples who visited, Mrs. Hope?" prosecutor Irvin Orsay asked.

Reba answered the question, but the names meant nothing to Syl. Reba said that after they were all cleaned up, she sat in the kitchen with the other two women, and her husband and the men went out to the garage. After a while, the men came in and announced they were going to the Rondack, a members-only bar and restaurant in Woodstock where white people went. Being white was an unspoken but understood requirement for admission.

"I told him to think again," Reba testified. "I thought maybe they were going to find James White. Not that it wouldn't be warranted." At that, there was stirring and murmuring in the courtroom. The judge banged her gavel. After things quieted down, which took about a minute, Reba continued with her testimony. She said her husband assured her that they were only going to the Rondack.

"I said to Paul, 'With a fat lip and blackening eye?' He gave me the 'I'm a big boy' look, so I left him alone. God, I wish I'd put up more of a fuss." The other two gentlemen said they'd drop their wives off at home and meet Paul at the Rondack, she added.

Reba testified that after twelve-thirty rolled around and her husband wasn't home, she called the Rondack. The bartender said that her husband was still there, telling everyone about the evening's brawl. Reba felt relieved to hear Paul was there and in good spirits. So she took some aspirin, poured herself a short brandy, settled in to watch TV in the den, and eventually fell asleep on the couch.

Reba told the court that around five o'clock the next morning, she was awakened by their youngest daughter, who'd snuggled up against her on the couch. That's when she realized that she hadn't heard her husband come in. En route to the kitchen door that opened out to the garage, Reba saw from the window that her husband's white Corvette was parked about halfway between the road and their house.

"When I squinted"—she performed a reenactment, craning her neck forward—"I could see Paul's arm hanging out of the driver's side window. Almost the way it might dangle if he was taking a break between cigarette drags. Paul quit smoking eight years ago, when our third daughter was born."

"What did you see next?" Orsay asked.

"I watched for, I don't know, a minute," she said. "Or two. I didn't see him move. No movement at all. So I thought he was drunk out of his mind and needed waking up. But I was just glad he'd made it back to our property without running into a ditch or a tree or another driver."

"What happened next?" Orsay prompted.

Reba's face balled up, as though just the thought of what she was about to describe gave her physical pain. Syl looked at Fate and he tapped her forearm and mouthed, *Breathe.*

"I threw something on and walked out to wake him up and help him inside, and as I got closer, I saw the blood on the door."

"Where *exactly* did you first see blood? Which door?" Orsay asked.

"The driver's side door."

"Where else?"

She started to shake her head rapidly. "The windshield. Inside. Somehow, I hadn't noticed it at first. Probably because of the fog. But lots of blood. So much. On the driver's side door." She was crying now, trying to talk through hiccups. "There was a lot on his hands, too."

"On Paul's hands?"

Reba gasped for air and said, "Yes. *Everywhere.* It seemed at the time, blood was just *everywhere.*"

"What did you do then?"

"I took a few more steps toward the car, called out his name, looked inside, and I just screamed." She clutched one of her lapels as though it might escort her safely through the memory. "I don't remember much of what happened between that and the police arriving."

The bailiff—he also worked part-time at the hardware store on Main Street—passed her a box of tissues.

"Who called the police, Mrs. Hope?"

"Tara did. She—"

"Your daughter Tara?" Orsay asked.

"Yes. Our eldest."

"I know this is hard for you, ma'am, but can you tell the court what you saw in the car?"

If Syl hadn't heard about it from other people who'd heard about it from people who knew the police officers who'd seen it and the coroner, she wouldn't believe the words that came from

Reba Hope's mouth. But now, knowing what Josey had done to the Black people he'd murdered, it all made sense.

"My husband was sitting upright in the seat, and on the dashboard and on his lap, there were—" She gasped, cried more. Everyone waited, patiently. The courtroom had gone so quiet, Syl was certain she heard a mouse moving in the walls.

"Whenever you're ready, Reba," Orsay said.

"I'm no doctor, but there was no mistaking what I saw. My husband's organs had been taken out of his body."

A woman sitting in the row in front of Syl and Fate burst into tears, jumped up, and ran out of the courtroom. Others whispered, covered their mouths, or shouted, "Oh, Jesus!" or "My God!"

"Animals!" a man behind Syl yelled out to James and Ella. *Who could blame him?* Syl thought. With the Hopes having been fresh off that fight with the Whites at the drive-in, stacked up next to what Ella had shouted at the gas station mini-mart attendant, what were people supposed to believe? Circumstantial or not.

"Order!" Judge Berk yelled.

James and Ella sat at two separate tables, alongside their attorneys. From what Syl could observe, they weren't allowed to have any direct contact with each other. Syl couldn't see their faces.

Judge Berk pulled off her glasses, set them down in front of her, stood up, and said, "There will be no more outbursts. You all knew what this case was about before coming here today. Stay home if you can't handle it. We'll now take a thirty-minute recess."

After the break, Reba was back on the stand to be questioned by the defense attorney, Solomon Ashby—an energetic man half

Orsay's age with pitch-black hair cut in U.S. Navy style. Ashby, Fate noted to Syl, looked sly but probably wasn't at all. He was at least six feet tall and wore a blue pin-striped suit that Fate said he'd bet was custom-made. And he wore gold wire-framed glasses, which he had to keep pushing up his nose.

"Mrs. Hope," Ashby said, standing still and straight in front of the witness stand. "Would you characterize your marriage as a happy one?"

"Yes," she said without hesitation. Syl could tell Reba was lying because she gazed down at her lap as she answered the question. And an honest woman with marital troubles might have said, *We weren't perfect, but we loved each other.*

"Any issues with infidelity between the two of you?" Ashby asked.

"In the past, yes."

"On whose part, Mrs. Hope?"

"We both had affairs, but we stopped. Well, I continued to hear that Paul had women in the city, but don't they all?"

"Are you saying you were okay with him possibly having affairs with other women?"

"I was not *okay* with it," she said impatiently, shifting in her chair. "I just didn't see any evidence that he was still cheating. I was too busy with my children to go looking for it. Listen, Paul was a good man. He made mistakes. We both did. I—I loved him, and he loved me. Of that I am certain."

"Mrs. Hope, when, approximately, did your last affair end?"

She rubbed her temples, looking down into her lap. When she lifted her head again, her eyes were closed.

"About a year ago," she said, eyes still shut.

"With whom did you have an affair, Mrs. Hope?"

She opened her eyes and said, "Andrew Parker, my husband's former business partner."

The judge had to bang her gavel again at the uproar.

Paul Hope was a founding partner of Hope, Wells & Parker, an accounting firm in Manhattan. They handled the books for large companies and personal estates owned by some of New York's richest families. People with money so old, even they didn't know how it had been made—or so they claimed.

Reba, a librarian, had grown up in a small town outside New Orleans and was from a well-off family, Mrs. Talbot told Syl during the trial. Reba had attended New York University, and she'd worked briefly for the New York Public Library before becoming a mother. After their second child was born, Paul agreed to build Reba a home in Connecticut or upstate to raise their growing family. She had chosen Saugerties for its mountain views and for the ways it reminded her of her hometown. Reba wanted a quiet country life for her and her children.

"Did your husband become aware of the affair?" Ashby asked.

"He did."

"When did Mr. Hope become aware of it, and how did he react?"

"A month or so before the Whites killed him."

"Mrs. Hope, careful," Judge Berk said. "Strike that," she instructed the stenographer.

Reba looked at Ashby and said, "He confronted me about the affair over Memorial Day weekend. He was very upset, but accepted it as punishment for having slept with someone I'd believed to be a dear friend, and we reconciled quickly."

"When was the last time you saw Mr. Parker? Privately, I mean."

"I can't recall," she said.

"I'll ask it another way. Were you or were you not with Mr. Parker just a few weeks ago, at a hotel in Hudson, New York?"

"Objection!" Orsay yelled.

"Overruled," the judge said. "Mrs. Hope, answer the question, please."

Syl glanced at Fate, whose lips had parted with disbelief.

Reba began to cry again. "I know what you're trying to do, and—"

"Answer the question, Mrs. Hope," the judge said calmly.

"Yes," Reba said. "I was with Andrew a few weeks ago."

Someone in the courtroom said, "I knew it," just a little too loud, and Judge Berk called for order. When the courtroom was nearly silent again, Mr. Ashby asked, "Is it true that you met Andrew Parker at a hotel a couple of days before your husband was murdered?"

"Yes, but I swear to God, on my daughters' lives and my own, I had nothing to do with Paul's murder! He was my best friend!"

The courtroom hummed with whispers again.

"Order!" the judge said.

"Andrew and I were only having sex!"

The defense attorneys weren't able to come up with anything solid to further support that theory. Though things still looked bad for James and Ella, no one forgot about the affair between Reba Hope and Andrew Parker.

CHAPTER EIGHT

As Syl was about to leave her house to join Mrs. Talbot's party, she thought how frustrating it was that the Whites had returned to Fervent that same day, stealing some of Mrs. Talbot's hard-earned attention. Not only had Mrs. Talbot accomplished a first sale, she'd sold a house in an all-white neighborhood in Kingston to a Black family—which was ironic, given that after the Whites went to prison and Mrs. Talbot became a widow, she was the only white person living in Fervent.

Fervent, an offshoot of Saugerties, was a hamlet with only twelve homes and a post office the size of a tool shed. Fervent wasn't an island, exactly, but similar. Ten of the houses were owned by Black families. The Talbots and the Whites were the only two white families in Fervent when Syl, Reggie, and their children arrived.

Just a few days after the Upshaws moved to Fervent, Mrs. Talbot told Syl that in the early '60s, a quartet of brothers with the last name of Fervent, all contractors and developers, had built nine identical houses, which sold quickly. So the brothers built three more, but changes in the economy caused the houses to sit empty for several months. Eventually, a Black couple (the Bellwoods, now living in Florida with their youngest daughter) made an offer on one of the vacant homes, bought it, and moved in.

Two other Black families followed suit. It wasn't long before most of the white residents started moving to Kingston or Woodstock or wherever they could find all-white neighborhoods, and it was Black people who bought their homes, and at good prices.

It's funny what one can get for a steal when white people are fleeing a place.

"Good riddance," Mrs. Talbot had said about one of the former neighbors. "Judith gossiped *far* too much, and her husband was always trying to sell us some kind of kitchen appliance or gadget. Electric knives and choppers, toasters that could hold ten slices of bread. What would Grant and I need with a toaster that browns ten slices at once? Anyway, they were annoying."

When Syl finally made it to Mrs. Talbot's, she was surprised to see the house was still full. Walls were being held up by neighbors, a few of Mrs. Talbot's local family members, ladies from her bridge and bingo groups, other realtors, and people Syl didn't recognize. GiGi and RJ were nowhere to be found. Syl hoped they'd actually gone in and offered congratulations. Syl gave Mrs. Talbot a hug, and she was about to sit and talk with her for a few minutes, but Mrs. Talbot was distracted by more visitors ringing the doorbell.

"Syl," Suzy John said from behind. "I hope RJ won't be mad at me."

"Mad about what?" Syl asked, turning to face her. Suzy, as usual, was nervously fiddling with the cross that hung from her beaded necklace.

"He and my boys were talking, and RJ brought up that godforsaken Josey man. *Demon* is what I *should* be calling him." She closed her eyes for a moment. "Anyway, I asked RJ not to utter that man's name. He looked a little ticked off with me."

"He'll survive," Syl said, moving away from Suzy as quickly, and politely, as she could. Suzy was always at the ready to give a mini sermon or Bible study session. Syl was rarely in the mood for that, and certainly wasn't now. In fact, she found herself eager to slip out. She really didn't want to speak with anyone or talk about the Whites or Josey. Syl caught Mrs. Talbot by the wrist and said, "Let's go out to a bar next week, after I get the children off to Georgia."

"I'll hold you to it, sweetie," Mrs. Talbot said, clasping Syl's hand. Her bouffant looked as though it had been styled only five minutes ago. "I know you're running from Suzy, so I won't stand in your way. Call me tomorrow?"

"Sure will," Syl said. She and Mrs. Talbot gave each other a hug. "Congratulations again, boss lady!"

In Fervent, everyone lived a decent life, though they were not a perfect community. There were riffs and tiffs. There were people who smiled a little too widely at someone else's spouse, people who didn't place a congratulatory or sympathetic phone call when everyone else did, daughters who turned up pregnant by a neighbor's home-from-college-for-the-holiday son. But Fervent was mostly quiet.

Or it had been before Christopher Josey and his nephew passed through Saugerties and changed everything.

Christopher Josey, a bulky brown-haired, green-eyed man with a penchant for terrorizing and taking the lives of Black people, had killed many before, and a few after, killing Paul Hope. Most of his heinous crimes were committed in various parts of northern

New York: Buffalo and Troy, in particular. He had also released his fury on Black people in other states. But the murder he committed on Long Island was the one for which he was caught. That's when he confessed to having killed Paul Hope. Josey's nephew, Samuel Foust, was also sentenced to life in prison for his part in Josey's crimes.

When Paul Hope's car was examined, two pieces of evidence were immediately visible: someone had opened the passenger door with a bloody hand and had tried to wipe the prints away, and there was a long blond hair—aside from Paul, who had short hair, none of the Hopes were blond—hanging from a thread on the passenger headrest. The prosecutor wove a tale about how Ella White had jumped into the car with Hope and held a gun to his head or a knife at his throat, all to keep Hope from running away. Then, the theory followed, James opened the driver's side door and took Hope's life.

Josey confessed to Paul Hope's murder unprovoked. He wanted all the glory, since he knew he'd likely be killed in prison or executed by the state of New York. In a tape-recorded statement, he described things about Hope's murder that hadn't been released to the public. Details only the coroner and mortician could have known. Even with that information, however, the authorities feared that Josey might be making a false confession. It was commonplace among serial offenders. So they sent a pair of crime-scene detectives to speak with Sam Foust, who, terrified, had tried to end his own life in a Long Island jail cell by banging his head against the wall. He'd only fainted and given himself a large bump. When told that his uncle had confessed to Paul Hope's murder, Sam offered up frightening details—ones that involved vital organs and a hunting knife. He also described the types of rocks the Hopes had used on their driveway. He said those pebbles were in Josey's car, and in the soles of their shoes, for days.

In the tape-recorded confession, Christopher Josey confirmed that he hadn't known Paul Hope personally.

"Well, what was your motive, Chris?" the interviewer asked Josey. "Your victims haven't *ever* been white, or people with much money, for that matter. You must've had a reason for going after Paul Hope."

"Did I tell you how pretty you are, miss?" Josey asked the interviewer.

"Yes, you did," she said. "Did you have a specific reason for killing Paul Hope?"

"Oh yeah, I had a reason," he said. "It was kinda silly, to be honest with ya. I saw him earlier that evening and asked him for a few bucks for gas."

"Hold on," the interviewer said. "You had a conversation with Paul Hope earlier on the day you killed him?"

"Sure did," Josey said. "He looked me up and down and mumbled 'Trash' when he walked away from me. Then I saw him late, late that night. Well, I guess it was morning when we saw him by hisself. I told Sam I wanted him on a goddamn platter. I didn't get the platter, but I cut him up good."

"Why did you take your victims' lives in such a gruesome manner? Why remove organs?"

Josey scoffed and said, "Hell, dude, I didn't *invent* it or anything. In England, kings had that done to people all the time. Do your reading." The interviewer wrote in her report that Josey then released a frightening, guttural laugh that made her eager to leave the room.

Josey's nephew, Foust, told his own lawyers and interviewers that he hadn't wanted to harm Hope.

"Chris forced me to help him with *that* one. None of it made much sense to me. He didn't kill other whites, usually. Break a jaw or an arm if he needed to. That's about it. We been called all sorts of things by other whites before. We ain't never *killed* 'em, though. But you just never know with Chris. So, I had to be ready for anything, all the time."

Josey told the interviewer that Hope's Corvette was hard to miss or forget. So when they saw it heading into Saugerties in the wee hours of the morning, he followed.

"Why were you in Saugerties?"

"I got a couple girls there that me and Sam see from time to time. That's all. No big mystery there for you to go trying to solve, rookie."

The authorities, while skeptical of Josey randomly killing a white man, had no choice but to accept the confession as true.

CHAPTER NINE

After leaving Mrs. Talbot's, and having eaten a plate of meatloaf—she added more ketchup to her helping, which was something Morgan had always done when she'd taken him some—Syl sat thinking.

"Jesus, I sure hope Morgan didn't write anything about our conversation in that journal of his," she whispered while refilling her glass with orange punch. Just then, GiGi and RJ came back in.

"Where'd you two go?" she asked. It wasn't a serious question. They couldn't have gone far on foot.

"Just down to the river with the John boys," GiGi said, heading for the kitchen cabinet that stored plates and bowls. "Are you eating now, maggot face?" she asked her brother, pausing before shutting the cabinet door.

"I'll get my own plate, bimbette," RJ replied. "I don't know where your hands've been."

"Both of you need to wash your hands," Syl said. "RJ, stop talking about Josey. And certainly not around Suzy John."

"Why not?" he asked as he waited for GiGi to finish at the spigot. "The newspapers are talking about him, and everybody else here in Fervent is too."

Syl rolled her eyes, put her plate in the sink, and sat back down at the table.

"I'm going to miss you two while you're in big-time Atlanta," she said, looking back and forth between them. "I want y'all to start packing tomorrow. None of that last-minute rushing like you did in December. Understand?" They both nodded. Syl warned them not to call asking her to ship this thing and that thing.

"Are you going to invite Mr. and Mrs. White to dinner sometime?" GiGi asked. "They *are* letting us come and get some of Morgan's records."

"I didn't invite them to dinner before they went to prison," she said. "Why would I start now?"

GiGi turned to her and looked as though she was about to say something, but she stopped short.

"What?"

"Nothing."

"Go ahead and say it, Gi."

"I think Mrs. White needs a close friend," GiGi said. "She's been through a whole lot, and I can't see any of the other mothers here in Fervent being as kind to her as you'd be. I know you two aren't Florida Evans and Willona Woods, but at least invite her over for coffee on the weekend, like you do with Fate. Or something."

RJ started shaking his head.

"Nah," he said with a smirk. Syl knew he was about to say something silly. "They might try to take her out for snitching."

GiGi tried to hold back her laugh but couldn't. And when she caught her breath, she said, "You're stupid."

"I'm through with the both of you," Syl said, shaking her head. She stood to leave the kitchen. Only GiGi stopped her.

"But seriously, Ma," she said. "Now that they're home, it's going to really hit them that Morgan's gone. And since you two aren't fighting over who would've raised him better, there's no more heat between you. Oh, and Mr. White lost his buddy when Mr. Talbot died."

"True, but—" RJ said. Syl and GiGi waited for him to finish his sentence.

"But?" Syl said.

"Well, Morgan *did* used to tell us all the time that they weren't as nice as everyone thought they were."

"You took the words right out of my mouth," Syl said to RJ. To GiGi, she said, "Yes, baby girl. They're grieving and went to prison for no reason. I feel all of that for them. But they've done other things that make me not want to be all cozy with them."

This reminded Syl of something Morgan had said when she and Fate told him the secret. Morgan had been vague, and she hadn't wanted to ask any questions.

"What did he tell you?" she asked RJ.

"He told us they used to make a lot of jokes. Mean ones about people. And that when they got into arguments about silly stuff, sometimes they fought."

"Fought?" Syl asked.

"Yep. Like a *fight* fight. See-you-at-three-o'clock-after-school kinda fights. Then make up and be all in love again, like nothing happened. He thought they were half crazy."

"He told me they stole sometimes, too," GiGi added. "Stole things from gas stations and stuff. For fun."

"Oh, Morgan told us his dad sometimes would wake up in the middle of the night," RJ said. "Walking up and down the hallways saying weird stuff, like he was sleepwalking, saying stuff like a soldier from when he was in World War One."

"It was Vietnam, dork," GiGi replied.

Syl recalled Mr. Talbot saying that James had been honorably discharged. Mr. Talbot had felt there was more to the story.

Syl studied her children for a minute while they ate meatloaf and the canned French-cut green beans she'd heated up. Neither of them seemed to want any of the white rice.

"Why haven't you two told me any of this before?" she chided.

GiGi shrugged and ate another forkful of meatloaf. RJ took a drink from his glass of cola.

"Four working ears and neither of you heard me ask that question?" Syl said.

"Because we aren't snit-ches," RJ said, drawing out the second syllable of *snitches.*

The two of them burst into laughter again.

"Stop it," Syl said. The children must have recognized the seriousness in her tone because they both went silent. "None of this is funny. Morgan was living with them and not feeling safe. He—"

"This is why we didn't tell you, Ma," RJ said. "Morgan was safe. He just thought they were cuckoo. That's all."

In the living room, Syl sat on the couch and fought back tears of anger and regret. She wished she had, years ago, asked Morgan more questions about his day-to-day life with Ella and James. She could've done something to make sure Ella and James were actually fit to raise the boy, and she knew at least half of Fervent's residents would have supported her.

Syl picked up a copy of *Jet* and propped her feet up on the wooden coffee table her neighbor and co-worker Hoke had made. She flipped several pages but wouldn't have been able to tell anyone what she'd seen on any of them. Her mind replayed what her children had just told her.

Damn. Fate is right.

CHAPTER TEN

When Syl first heard that the Whites were innocent of Hope's murder and soon to be released, she thought it was a joke. She was at Aco, counting boxes of miniature plastic tires—each one the size of a Cheerio—when Hoke walked up to her in a corner of the warehouse and blurted it out. He had been out in his car and heard about Josey's confession on the radio.

"Don't joke about stuff like that, Hoke. Did you book our room for Saturday? My kids'll be down in the city all day visiting cousins." Hoke—he preferred the nickname to his real name, Harold—had children, too. Dwight and Jamilla. They were both a couple of years younger than GiGi and RJ. Hoke and his wife were legally separated and living apart. His kids had chosen to stay with him because they didn't want to leave their school and friends to move to Paterson, New Jersey. So though Syl and Hoke didn't *have* to keep their relationship secret, they had agreed it would be best for their teens.

"I'm not joking, baby. Heard it on WHUD just now. James and Ella White are innocent and getting *out*."

Syl examined his face as well as she could, trying to find a hint of playfulness in his eyes, but he was serious.

"Wow" was all she could say. She was only half surprised to learn they were innocent of the murder, but she was shocked to learn that the real murderer had confessed.

"Glad the truth came out," Hoke said. "Going to prison for something you didn't do. Man—" He shook his head.

"Something larger than us is looking out for them, Hoke."

"Yeah," he said. "I still think something's a little off about James. I've never been able to put my finger on it. Either way, I hope they move somewhere else. Murderers or not."

"Me, too."

"And yes to your question," he said.

"What question?"

"I got our room." He looked around again, mocking caution, to see if anyone was nearby. Then he pulled her to him and kissed her. The kiss was a long, deep one. Any other day, Syl might have invited him to meet her in a boiler room. But images of Ella and James seemed to be stamped all around the warehouse. She wouldn't be able to enjoy herself with Hoke just minutes after learning the Whites were getting out of prison.

"Let's meet tonight, at our spot. And still meet on Saturday."

"No, Hoke. We just did that. You know how hard it is to explain to my nosy kids where I'm going at nine P.M.?"

"That's because they up in your business too damn much. See you around ten o'clock."

"No, you won't."

Hoke gave Syl another kiss and left the warehouse.

Syl had been certain Hoke had taken a liking to her long before either of their marriages failed. When their boys played softball in elementary school, Hoke always found a way to sit near Syl in the bleachers—if Reggie wasn't there. And at Aco, in front of the microwave station, he often commented on how good her food smelled and looked. But when Reggie left Syl for a high school classmate with whom he'd been having a long-distance affair—it sparked at a class reunion that Syl had had to miss because she had just been promoted to shipping and receiving supervisor—Hoke approached her one day in the parking lot as she was getting into her car.

"Listen," he said. "We both single now. Let's go out." She was so flattered by the invitation she nearly leapt out of the car and onto him.

"I'm *still* a married woman, Hoke," she reminded him, narrowing her eyes and half smiling.

"I'm still a married man, Syl. But we're single."

Syl had a type. Like Reggie, who was six-four, Hoke was also tall: six foot three. Both men looked like they could lift a small car without any help.

"Hmmm," she hummed. It was something she had picked up from her frequent conversations with Fate. "I won't be seen on a date until I'm divorced. I'm old-fashioned."

"Hmmm," he mocked. "If being seen is all you're worried about, we can go where nobody knows us, slick. Now, let me get going. Don't wanna keep Dwight and Morgan waiting. Think on it and let me know tomorrow."

"Is Morgan going with you two to that record store again?" Syl asked. "James and Ella are going to get jealous and put a hit out on you."

"I'm not paying James and Ella any mind," Hoke returned. "It's not my fault their son loves sixties soul and they don't know much about it."

"That's the truth," Syl said. Morgan didn't just like the music; he knew which groups had formed due to a split-off from another, which groups were blood relatives who'd once sung gospel, and so forth. "I think it's good of you to spend time with Morgan. He needs a Black man in his life who'll tell him little things he needs to know."

"We talk about more than music, of course, but whatever he needs, he knows he can come to me. I gotta go. Let me know about us tomorrow."

"Tomorrow?" She laughed out loud. A couple of their coworkers looked their way. Syl and Hoke both waved at them.

"You heard me, ladybug," he said. "Tomorrow." He reached out and rubbed her chin with a finger. "I'm a hot commodity out here. Don't you see the line?"

"Yeah, right," Syl joked. "You're a jive turkey. That's what you are." But he *was* a hot commodity. Almost every Black woman at Aco, married or not, giggled when Hoke greeted them. "Well, I have a line, too. Haven't you heard?"

"Alright, Patrice Rushen," he said, referring to one of Rushen's hits. "And stop saying 'jive turkey.' My kids say it's old."

"Teenagers think everything we do and say is old," Syl said. "Maybe we *are* old."

"You don't look it. I can tell you that," Hoke said, flashing a wide smile. "Okay, okay. I'll come up with some ideas and have them ready for you tomorrow."

"Whatever, Hoke," Syl said, fanning him off and watching him closely as he walked to his car.

"I'm serious," he shouted to her.

One week later, Syl told her children she was going to a coworker's birthday party and that she'd be home before eleven.

"On a Wednesday night?" GiGi asked. "Who has a birthday party on a Wednesday night?"

"Old people," RJ said.

She and Hoke drove, separately, to Poughkeepsie, where they had dinner and kissed passionately in the back seat of Syl's car. The week after that, on their second date, they got a room.

—

Within five or so minutes of Syl hearing the news about the Whites from Hoke, the assembly line stopped—everyone paused, debating and talking about the Whites' release. When Syl got home, she turned on *Channel 12 News*. There was segment after segment about it. She sank into her couch, watching and listening to the reporters. If she hadn't needed to cook dinner, she wouldn't have moved for hours.

"I could've been knocked over by a mothball when Hoke first told me," Syl said to Fate over the phone. She was biting the skin around her left thumbnail. For a fleeting moment she wondered if Morgan had visited one or both of the Whites to let them know he was looking for his birth parents, but she settled on it being highly unlikely. She didn't mention it to Fate.

"I can't believe they're getting out. They're going to slit all my tires and paint bad words on my house. I know it."

"They won't come back to Saugerties," Syl said. "Ella won't be able to stand all the whispering and strange looks. And we both know that'll never end, regardless of Josey's confession. Aside from coming here to clear their house out to sell it, we won't see them. Trust me."

Within a week of Josey's confession, Ella was released from Bedford Hills, a few hours before James was released from Attica. There had been a news conference outside Bedford Hills, just beyond its gates. Fate had seen the live airing of it. He'd been having lunch in the teachers' lounge when it came on.

"It reminded me of one of those press conferences before or after a major boxing match between champions, Syl," he said. "Cameras clicking, reporters galore. I can't even remember much about Ella's speech. Just her odd smile. Well, not a smile, exactly. But you know what I mean."

"She gave a whole speech?"

"Not a speech, but she said something to the effect of being glad the truth had come out, that she was sorry for what she, James, Morgan, and the Hopes had all gone through, how now she could properly grieve Morgan's passing. That type of thing. All I could think about was her and James coming to get me for that testimony I gave. Lord, Sylvia, why didn't I just keep my mouth shut on the stand? Why did I have to say all—"

"Fate. You were on a witness stand, in a court of law."

"I tattled. That's what I did. God, help me."

Syl thought back to what she could remember of him being questioned by the prosecutor.

"Mr. Jolly," Orsay had said. "Tell the court where you live and what you do for a living."

"I live in Saugerties, in the hamlet of Fervent," Fate replied, blinking rapidly, as he did when under pressure. "I teach at River Hudson High School." His back was straight, and with a handkerchief he wiped sweat from his face and neck. Fate was wearing a black suit, a white shirt, and a black tie. Syl had warned him that he might want to forgo the tie and the jacket. It would be more comfortable, she had suggested.

"How do you know the defendants, James and Ella White?"

"We are neighbors."

"Ella White was a colleague of yours at River Hudson High, is that correct?"

"Yes, sir."

Orsay went on asking questions to which he already knew the answers: What was Ella's role at the school, and how many houses were in between Fate's house and the Whites'? Fate seemed to relax slightly. But Syl worried that as the questions got less general, he might tense up again.

"Did you have to interact with Mrs. White very much at River Hudson High, Mr. Jolly?"

"Yes, sir. At least a few times a week, in the main office."

"Would you characterize those interactions as pleasant, amicable?"

Fate hesitated, then said yes.

"That's interesting, Mr. Jolly, because many of your colleagues mentioned that you often complained of feeling mistreated by Mrs. White in the workplace *and* in your neighborhood."

Having been caught in that tiny white lie, Fate went into a frenzy of truth telling. The whole truth and nothing but the truth, so help him God. Syl wished she could run up and sit with him, hold his hand while he testified. Her own testimony had lasted five or six minutes. She had been asked only about the injury she'd received as a result of James throwing a toy against a wall.

Fate used his hand as a fan as he told the story about how James and Ella had yelled at him for cutting his grass at ten o'clock on a Saturday morning.

"I asked them why I was being singled out," Fate said, nearly in tears and speaking so quickly that Orsay told him he could take his time. "Thank you, sir." He took a deep breath, but it didn't calm him much at all. "I pointed out that one of our other neighbors had started cutting his lawn an entire hour before I had. And *that* neighbor did his weed whacking *first.* Have you ever heard a weed whacker at eight-thirty on a Saturday morning? There's no going back to sleep after that. I'm usually awake by seven, anyway. But you know what I mean."

"What did the Whites say when you'd pointed out their—" Orsay seemed to be searching for the right word or phrase. "Their singling you out, as you put it?"

"They both just stood there, staring at me, faces pinched as though they smelled something putrid."

"What happened next?"

Fate looked down at his lap for a moment. When he lifted his head, Syl could see the glisten on his cheeks from his tears. "James charged at me, grabbed me by my throat, and said, 'Don't get sassy, fudge packer. You're lucky I don't beat you to a pulp right this second.'"

Some people in the courtroom gasped; others stirred and whispered.

"Then?"

"I kicked, swung my arms, and moved as best I could, but I couldn't get him to let me go."

"Was your breathing restricted, Mr. Jolly?"

"Of course it was." He was overcome with sobbing.

"Do you need a five-minute recess, Mr. Jolly?" Judge Berk asked him.

"No, ma'am," he replied quickly. "I mean, Your Honor. I'd like to get this over with."

The judge nodded and leaned back in her chair.

"I thought James was going to *kill* me, right there in my front yard, in broad morning light."

"Do you recall what caused him to release your neck?"

"My neighbor Mrs. Francine Griffith came running out of her house and yelled for James to release me. Well, she didn't exactly run. She was about eighty-seven or eighty-eight at the time. God rest her sweet soul. But she came out of her house making a fuss at James. I believe that woman saved my life."

"And did he release you immediately after Mrs. Griffith appeared?"

"No, sir," Fate answered. "It wasn't Mrs. Griffith's showing up that made him release me. It was only when Ella said, 'Let's go, James,' that he let me go."

"Mr. Jolly, did you say Ella White said, 'Let go, James'?"

"No, sir. Ella said, '*Let's* go, James.' Then he released my neck, pushed me to the ground, spit really close to my head, and said—" Fate stopped, shook his head, and covered his face.

"What did James White say, Mr. Jolly?"

"He told me that if I started my mower before noon again, he'd remove my genitalia, for starters, and inflict other awful physical harms." There was more stirring in the courtroom.

"Would I be right to assume that the defendant used . . . different language than what you just have?"

"Yes, sir," Fate confirmed. "He was vulgar."

"Did you ever receive an apology from either of the defendants for that incident, Mr. Jolly?"

"I did," Fate replied. "A few days later. But it wasn't genuine. It was Grant Talbot who told them he'd heard from Mrs. Griffith what had happened. Mr. Talbot shamed them into apologizing. They knocked on my door one Sunday afternoon. I only cracked the door open and kept the chain latched. They had the nerve to bring flowers. *Flowers.* Ella did all the talking. Well, most of it, at least."

"Do you recall any of what she said?"

"Something about them being under a lot of stress and that James hadn't been sleeping well, having migraines and all that. Anyway, she started crying and tried to hand me the flowers. I said, 'I don't want the flowers, Ella. I just want you two to treat me like a human being, the same way you treat everyone else here in Fervent.' I ended up taking the flowers, but I gave them to the Talbots because I figured they had been the reason for the apology."

"What did James White say when they came to your porch?"

"He said five words. I remember it like yesterday. 'Sorry, Fate. I mean it.'"

But a year after the incident, after Syl had moved to Fervent and befriended Fate, they were at a community cookout hosted by Mr. and Mrs. Talbot when she witnessed a hostile conversation between Ella and Fate.

A group of the neighborhood teens had surrounded Fate, complaining about other teachers at the high school. Fate didn't want to encourage the kids' venting about his colleagues, so he redirected the conversation by asking the rising seniors what their plans were for after graduation. Were they going straight to college? If so, to which colleges were they planning to apply?

"I don't think I'll need college, Mr. Jolly," Morgan said. Whereas most of the teens his age had worn shorts and T-shirts to the picnic, Morgan had on khaki slacks and a plain white button-down shirt. He always stood apart, though Syl didn't believe he was trying to. In many ways, Morgan was a straight arrow. But he rebelled in a few subtle ways. Refusing to cut his thick mane of hair was one of them. James hated his cornrows. Ella liked them, and Syl had heard her tell people a couple of times that she just couldn't seem to get her fingers to braid them right. Morgan added, "I've done research and I've found that a four-year college degree, for some career paths, just sucks up time that could be better spent getting real on-the-job experience."

"For example?" Fate asked.

"My shift managers at Kmart probably make more money than *you*. No offense."

"None taken."

"They don't have college degrees," Morgan said. "Even our regional manager is *sans* degree."

"What would you like to do *sans* a college degree? Interested in retail management?"

"Yes. I think I'd be very good at it. And I enjoy it. It's actually not very difficult. It's all about planning, and supply and demand. Of course, there's the whole dealing-with-people thing, which, fine. I'll get better at that in time."

Syl heard Fate say to Morgan, "I tell everyone to at least give college a try, if they have the grades to get in. And try not to pay any tuition, if you can avoid it. But you seem to have a plan, young brother." Morgan wasn't much for smiling, but Syl could tell by how his shoulders relaxed, and by the fact that he started eating from the plate he'd been holding in his hand, that he felt recognized in the conversation. Fate continued, telling Morgan about many people he knew who'd never been to college but were doing very well in life, making great salaries. Ella and James walked up to them as Fate said, "I respect you, brother, for not wanting to go to college *just* because it's what most other people do right after high school."

Syl, still standing nearby, took note of James's and Ella's crossed arms and pensive facial expressions.

An hour or so later, while Syl and others were starting to wrap up the food and shift into playing games, she saw Ella walk over to Fate, who was sitting alone, sipping a cup of punch and fidgeting with his shirt's tail.

"May I speak with you for a minute, in the front yard? For privacy," Syl managed to make out over the chatter. Fate uncrossed his legs, stood up, and followed Ella.

Syl thought this was strange, so she wandered toward the front yard herself. She heard Ella say, "Stop calling Morgan *brother.* As a matter of fact, just stay away from our son, you, you—"

"Instead of searching for some insult to hurl at me, maybe take a moment and think about why you need to do so at *all.* I've done nothing to you, Ella. Absolutely *nothing.* I thought we agreed to move forward. No more of this tension and—"

"Morgan doesn't need to hear stories about the types of people you're probably talking about. Your *friends* and what weird, disgusting ways they make a living because they can't get *regular* jobs."

Syl was about to turn the corner and give Ella a piece of her mind, but one of the neighbors' toddlers hugged Syl's leg from behind, startling her. Syl picked the little boy up and bounced him on her hip as his mother approached. But all the while, she watched and listened.

"Weird? Disgusting?" Fate shot back. "Ella, you don't even know the people I was referring to or what they do for a living. If you'd asked, I would have told you that I was talking about people such as—"

"Save it. Just keep away. Or you'll have to deal with *my* hand around your throat, not James's. And *I* won't let go."

Fate dropped his arms to his sides. "Threatening me, Ella? Again? You've got a lot of hate in your heart. What have I ever done to you and your family except show kindness?"

Ella didn't reply.

"Exactly," Fate said. "Not a damn thing."

With her hip baby-free, Syl walked toward them and said, "I wasn't going to get mixed up in this, but, Ella, I can't stand and listen to you tal—"

"Then *don't* get mixed up in it, and go back around to the party," Ella said.

"Who the hell you think you're talking to?" Syl asked.

"This is about *my* son, Sylvia. *My* son."

"Everyone in town knows Morgan is your son. But it takes a village, and you just happen to be living in a village full of Black people. If you gon' get pissed every time one of us gives Morgan some advice, or even shows him some care, maybe move some damn where else."

Ella folded her arms across her chest and stormed off toward her own house.

"You alright?" Syl asked Fate, who looked defeated.

"Yeah."

"I'm tired of her picking on you, Fate. I—"

"It's okay, Syl. I'm damn near used to it now."

"Well, get un-used to it. Fuck that."

Fate turned to walk away.

"Where are you going?" she called out. "You want to talk about it?"

Fate shook his head no and kept walking.

CHAPTER ELEVEN

The evening Syl, GiGi, and RJ went to the Whites', Syl first warned the children that she didn't want to stay for more than half an hour. She gave the excuse of not wanting to impose on the Whites, but the truth was that Syl simply didn't trust them. Thirty minutes would be plenty of time for the kids to flip through Morgan's albums while she exchanged pleasantries with James and Ella. Hopefully, they would mention whether or not they'd opened the box of things Morgan had taken to D.C.

She spoke to Fate a few minutes before leaving her house.

"If I don't call you within an hour, come to my house and check on us," she said, half joking.

"I will," he said. "You want me to come with you? They'll let me in. It'll look bad on them if they don't."

Syl thought about this offer for a few seconds and decided it wasn't a good idea.

"Okay, well," Fate suggested, "if you see *any* journals or diaries in Morgan's room, toss them in your purse and pretend you forgot to turn the stove off."

"I'm not doing that, silly," Syl said. "Morgan didn't write anything down about me, you, or the secret."

"I'll remember that when you call me from the emergency room."

"Boy, hush. Call my house in an hour if you don't hear from me first."

When Syl and the children were welcomed into the Whites' house by Ella, it smelled of cinnamon and white vinegar. Syl knew the old household trick. The combination, boiled together, then left to simmer on low, got rid of smells that aerosols couldn't. She imagined the house must have smelled stale and shut up when they'd reentered.

"Come on in, guys," Ella said with mild cheer. Syl could tell Ella had been crying, and she almost asked if they should visit on another day. But at the same time, Syl wanted the visit to be over with. The kids would go through the records, choose a few while Syl and Ella made small talk, and then they'd go back home. "GiGi and RJ, you two go on in his room. James and I already went through the two crates that are on his bed. Why don't you both take four or five records each? For now, I mean." She reminded them that, in time, she'd give them more. "Sylvia, would you join me in the kitchen? I was in the middle of washing more of our dusty dishes."

The Whites' kitchen looked like an indoor yard sale that featured only plates, bowls, glasses, and mugs. The counters were covered with them, as was half of the square table, which sat in the center of the room.

"Have a seat," Ella said. To Syl, she looked as though she hadn't slept since her visit two days prior. "Gosh, can I get you a glass of water or something? I don't have much else except some flat soda."

"No, I'm fine. Thanks, though."

Watching Ella return to the sink filled with sudsy steaming

water made Syl think of her own mother, and what she would've done in that moment. But just as she was about to ask if there was anything she could do to help, Ella turned to her, wiped the sweat from her forehead with her forearm, and said, "I sent James out to buy paint. Neither of us has been in the best of moods today, but he's been on a tear. Some shade of white. I told him to buy a few cans of some shade of white for the living room and hallway." Ella seemed delirious. "Sylvia, I have a hankering for clam chowder. Isn't that something? It's eighty-six degrees out there and I want soup. How about that? How are you?"

Just as Syl was about to give a stock reply—*I'm doing fine. Just trying to make it*—she noticed the box on the floor in one corner of the kitchen. What caught her attention wasn't so much the box itself as the bright orange tape that had once sealed it shut. The top of Morgan's gray backpack was peeping out. "Everything's okay," Syl said, and Ella turned back to the sink. "Just trying to get these two ready for their dad's."

A sensation Syl hadn't felt since she was nine or ten years old crept around in her stomach and made her arms tingle. It was pure mischief. Had the box been next to her, she would've looked in.

"They leave tomorrow, right?"

"Yes," Syl said, eyeing the box.

"You'll be an empty nester before you know it, Sylvia."

"I know," Syl said, suddenly aware of what those words must mean to Ella, whose only child was gone forever. If Morgan were alive, he would probably be there helping Ella with the stacks of dishes. He was quite the helper. Syl attempted to change the subject. The topic of work might be more suitable, she thought. Fate would be proud of her for finding out whether or not Ella planned to return to RHH. “Spoken to anyone at the high school yet? Planning on going back to your old—”

“Sylvia, we need to talk about something.” Ella dried her hands and leaned against her counter. “I have not always been kind to you, when all you were trying to do was help Morgan. At the time, I just couldn’t see it that way. I wanted to say this at your house the other day, but not in front of the kids. I am sorry. I really am.”

Syl was taken aback.

“Oh. Well, thanks,” she said. “I’m just glad you know it was never meant to hurt your feelings. I probably could’ve come to you differently than I did, and—”

“You were just being neighborly. Like you once said, it takes a village,” Ella said. “Which reminds me: I have something just for you.” Ella walked to the table, took a burgundy leather wallet from her pocketbook, and pulled out a small photograph. It was a school picture of Morgan from when he was in the ninth or tenth grade. “Do you remember that sweater he’s wearing?” She handed the photograph to Syl, who looked at it and put her hand over her mouth.

“I sure do,” she said. “We gave that to him as a birthday gift.” Morgan had joined her and the kids on a trip down to the city to get them new school clothes. He had admired the beige cardigan with red stitching and buttons, so, without his knowing, she had bought it. She and the children kept it a secret until it was time to give it to him.

A teardrop landed on the photograph. She hadn’t even realized she was crying.

“You can have that picture,” Ella said, tears running down her cheeks. “If I find a larger version of it, I’ll give it to you.”

“Thank you, Ella. Thanks so much.”

The two mothers held each other's gaze for a few seconds.

Just then there was the sound of something crashing to the floor down the hallway, and RJ yelled, "It's okay. Nothing's broken."

Ella frowned and hurried toward Morgan's room. Syl moved to follow her, then stopped.

She darted over to the box. Next to the backpack, which was zipped closed, were a pair of sneakers and a wallet. There was no journal in sight, which meant it must still be in the backpack.

Syl walked to the kitchen's threshold to make sure Ella was still occupied with the children. Then, with large, galloping steps, she hustled back to the box, unzipped Morgan's bag, and there it was, a spiral-bound journal just like GiGi's, except black instead of yellow. Syl opened it and turned toward the end, hoping to see dates that coincided with when she'd told him his truth, but there were no dates there. This gave her some relief. It was unlikely that he'd written about their conversation at all.

Just as Syl was about to drop the journal back into the bag and zip it up, it occurred to her that if James and Ella had opened the journal, they likely wouldn't have returned it to the backpack. *They haven't read it yet,* she realized. So, with trembling fingers, Syl gently flipped to see where the entries ended. He had almost used the whole book.

Syl, you can't do this, she thought. *Ella was so kind to you just now.*

But Syl knew that if there was so much as a sentence in the journal about her telling Morgan the secret, she would feel the Whites' wrath. Anyone the Whites would tell might distrust Syl, too. So Syl held the journal close to her body, turned herself away from the doorway, and tore several pages from the back of it. With each gentle tear, she coughed and feigned sneezing. Once she had two chunks of at least twenty pages in hand, she folded them and stuck each portion, along with the frizzy ends, into her pocketbook. Then she put the journal back in its rightful place, zipped up the bag, and went down the hall to Morgan's bedroom, where Ella, GiGi, and RJ were silently putting the last records back into the old wooden crate.

Ella wished GiGi and RJ a great summer and told them she was sorry they'd miss the upcoming memorial walk in Morgan's honor.

"But like we talked about, you two can go to the trail anytime and sit and think of him," Ella said.

"We will, Miss Ella," GiGi said. The teens both gave Ella a hug.

Once out of the Whites' yard, Syl said, "I'm going to walk over to Fate's and see what he's doing. You two need to go double-check your suitcases."

"How many times you want us to check 'em? Dang," RJ said.

Syl, carrying what could save her and Fate a world of trouble, was a bundle of nerves. She wasn't in the mood for talk-back.

"Do as I say. Period."

The children looked at her as though she'd grown a second head, and they walked to the house.

Fate met Syl at his front door. He had obviously been watching from his window.

"What happened? Come on in."

Once inside, Syl said, "I feel like I'm gon' throw up, or shit, or both." She had to do neither, though her body ached with fear, excitement, and guilt for taking the pages.

"Go to the bathroom then!"

"I'm okay," she said. "But, Fate—" She couldn't find the words to tell him what she'd just done.

"What's wrong? You're acting loony." She reached into her purse and pulled out the two portions of pages. One of the frizzies floated to the floor. "Syl, no you *didn't*!" he shouted.

"I did, Fate."

"How? What in the— Girl! You. You— So, did he write down what you told him, and that it came from you?"

"We 'bout to find out."

As they walked to Fate's kitchen table, Syl explained how she got the pages.

"Did you get a chance to look at them at *all*?" Fate asked.

"Not really."

Syl took the two batches of paper back from Fate and started to lay them out on the table. There were pages of D.C. phone numbers and addresses, with only first names written alongside them. The concluding pages had more short lists, most of which appeared to be lists of museums and monuments. "See, this page is dated months before he went to D.C., so he didn't even use the journal much, it seems," she said.

Fate scanned the table and said, "Yeah, and he didn't date most of them."

After a few beats of silence, Syl turned to Fate and said, "Feels strange, looking at his handwriting and knowing he's gone. Lord, it still makes no sense to me that he's gone. Maybe God thought he was suffering." Fate rubbed her back and hugged her.

About thirty minutes later, Syl relaxed onto Fate's couch and said, "Thank *God.* We don't have to worry about that anymore. Jesus Christ, I'm gon' sleep so good tonight."

"Sho nuff!" Fate said.

"You're so country," Syl said. She felt a smile settle effortlessly on her face.

"I need a drink. Shit!"

"Me, too," Syl said to Fate's back as he walked toward his

kitchen. He returned with two cans of Coors and two glasses. "I don't need that glass."

For at least two minutes, they drank from their cans in silence.

"You didn't see another notebook in the bag or box, did you?" Fate asked.

"Nope."

"Then he was discreet till the end. We're in the clear."

"We're all good, brother."

"They still probably want my head on a spike for my testimony, though."

Syl, feeling at ease, told Fate to stop worrying about that. Ella and James had bigger fish to fry, she said. "Like getting jobs."

CHAPTER TWELVE

One week after Syl tore the pages from Morgan's journal, most of the Fervent residents, Syl and Fate included, joined James and Ella on a nature trail walk in Cairo to memorialize Morgan. Syl and Fate rode to Cairo together in his car. There seemed to be an unspoken agreement between the two friends that they wouldn't talk much. For Syl, it was like attending Morgan's graveside service all over again. But since it was Fourth of July weekend, seeing some people out in the yards cleaning their charcoal grills and testing firecrackers made a slight difference.

Syl knew Fate had been right when he had reminded her—several times—that she hadn't forced Morgan to take that trip to D.C. Still, during the ride to Cairo, she couldn't help but think that if she hadn't told Morgan the secret, there might not be a memorial trail walk for Morgan.

Syl and Fate were the last to arrive. She didn't take a head count, but if she had to guess, she'd say there were twenty to twenty-five of her neighbors there. Hoke was in a cluster with Curt and Peaches Bainbridge. Mrs. Talbot was in a circle with the Whites and the Flemings.

The temperature was in the high seventies, and it had been breezy off and on all morning. As Syl and Fate approached their neighbors, the trees, lush with green foliage, seemed to shake slightly, announcing their arrival.

"Good morning, latecomers," Peaches Bainbridge sang out. Peaches was dressed like one of those women in a '60s coffee commercial. Pleated linen dress with a starched collar. She wore flats instead of sneakers.

Syl could tell Fate was eager to break the silence he'd maintained on the ride there.

"Peaches, you do know this is a nature *walk* and not a nature *stand*, don't you?" Fate said. Syl nearly choked trying not to laugh. Fate knew how to lighten a mood.

"Don't underestimate these shoes, jack," Peaches retorted playfully. "I can jog in these jokers if I want."

Peaches was easily the prettiest woman in Fervent, a dead ringer for the actress Brenda Sykes. She mostly wore her long, silky dark brown hair down and feathered, but for the combined nature walk and memorial, she had it pulled back into a bun. Syl had never been one to wish she had what her late mother referred to as "good hair," but when Peaches had a fresh wash and set, it was divine enough for Syl to consider buying a couple of wigs.

"It's probably in poor taste for me to speak about this, since we're here to honor their son," Peaches said. "But how do you two feel about those two being back in Fervent, permanently?" She threw her chin in the Whites' direction. The couple stood about ten feet away, hand in hand, talking to Mrs. Talbot.

"I don't love it," Syl replied. "But I guess Fervent's their home."

"Well, if I'm honest," Peaches began, "I think they should've waited longer to do this. Right now, everyone's probably just thinking about *their* mess and not Morgan. They probably should've just done this alone for now."

"I half agree, but they know we all loved him," Syl said.

"And isn't this the same trail the Talbots came to a lot?" Fate asked.

It was, Syl confirmed. It was the late Mr. Talbot's friendship with James that made Morgan aware of the trail, she reminded Fate and Peaches.

Peaches raised her eyebrows and scoffed.

"What? You know something we don't know?" Fate asked.

"From what I've heard, Old Man Talbot wasn't *too* impressed by James. He was quoted as saying Morgan was the more sensible one of the two, and that he—Mr. Talbot—felt as though he was always trying to talk sense into James instead of just having a friendly conversation."

Syl and Fate looked at each other, astonished. Syl had always assumed there was a bit of a father-son dynamic between the only two white men in Fervent—given their significant age difference—but she didn't know that Mr. Talbot had been exasperated with James.

"Who told you that?" Fate asked.

"A very, very reliable source."

"Mrs. April Talbot?" Fate said.

"I'm not telling."

"Yes, ma'am, you are," Fate retorted. "Spit it out."

"My husband told me," Peaches said. "He got it straight from Mr. Talbot's mouth. Long time ago."

"During the trial?" Syl asked.

"Long, long before any of that stuff happened," Peaches said. "And since we're talking, he—"

"Lord," Fate said to Syl. "She has more." To Peaches he said, "You're on a roll today, aren't you?"

"I guess I am. When they were convicted of the murder, Mr. T initially said he wouldn't put it past *either* of them. He knew about the Whites' fights and mean streaks."

"Well, at least we now know, for *sure,* they're innocent of *that,*" Syl said.

"I suppose so," Peaches said. "There's always the chance Reba Hope or that Parker man hired Josey."

"Josey would've said so," Fate said. "He'd have no reason to protect Reba Hope or Andrew Parker, or anyone else." Syl and Peaches nodded in agreement.

Syl and Fate made their way toward the Whites, greeting others as they walked by. Ella looked at Syl with what felt like judgment. Syl knew she and Fate had arrived a little late, but it was by fewer than five minutes.

"Good morning, Ella. James," Syl said. They both nodded. Syl decided not to make much of it. They were, after all, at a memorial walk for their son.

Syl noticed Suzy John standing off by herself. She, too, wore a faint scowl, but it was not directed toward Syl. It was Fate who Suzy was glaring at with contempt. He must have recently made her the butt of some joke. *Did he call her Olive Oyl again?* Syl wondered. Suzy was about five foot eleven and couldn't weigh more than one hundred twenty-five pounds. Anyone who tasted her decadent food wondered why she wasn't heavier. Suzy had had some culinary training but had quit the schooling to devote her life to ministry. Syl had helped her make potato salad for a picnic once, and she had been astonished by Suzy's skill with a knife.

Suzy John and Fate, for reasons Syl never quite understood, had an "I like you, I like you not" relationship. While Suzy was very religious, Syl never got the sense that Suzy and Fate's subtle rivalry had anything to do with Fate's being gay. Suzy always greeted Fate and Vincent kindly when she saw them walking around Fervent or in the grocery store. In fact, Suzy seemed to like chatting with Vincent.

"Are you two ready to begin the walk?" Mrs. Talbot asked the Whites.

"Yeah," James replied, taking Ella by the hand again. "Let's do it."

Syl had never known exactly what Morgan liked about the trail. She imagined it was the solitude it offered—since it was outside Saugerties. Syl had once asked her children if they understood why he preferred the Cairo trail, but they didn't know, either.

As people began to follow the Whites into the woods, they all walked up a slight incline. Alongside the dusty trail was a family of squirrels—some looking on cautiously, some chasing each other around an old stump. The shade from trees Syl believed to be oaks helped keep them cool, but Syl still broke a sweat. Her beige cotton blouse, though thin, was dotted with perspiration within five minutes. The few teenagers who'd come along—Syl wished GiGi and RJ were there—didn't seem bothered by the climb. Mrs. Talbot was obviously used to hiking, too. *Some nerve she has,* Syl thought. *To be in such good shape at seventy-five.*

"Girl, they didn't tell us they were giving us a *tour* of the trail," Fate said to Syl when she caught up to him. The two of them fell behind the group. James was still leading the way, pointing out one thing or another. This type of tree, that type of bird. Things he'd learned from Mr. Talbot, he said. Some of it he'd learned from Morgan, Ella added.

"Did you notice that?" Syl asked Fate.

"Notice what?"

"I spoke to the Whites and they looked at me like they wanted to douse my face in holy water."

"I was too busy trying not to look their way," he said. *Smart,* Syl considered. The moment they had walked up to the group, and after they had greeted the Whites, Fate had launched himself into conversation with other neighbors. "I wouldn't take it personal, Syl. Not today, at least."

"Of course. You're right," Syl said. But she'd seen them smile slightly at others. "Oh, before I forget: You and Suzy have words again?"

"Not today."

"What about this *week*?"

"Suzy's always mad at someone about something. But she might be stewing about yesterday." Fate related that Suzy's husband, Ervin, had walked over to Fate's to ask about the types of mulch he used in his flower beds. After the conversation had reached about ten minutes, Suzy yelled from her front porch for Ervin to come and help her with something. Ervin didn't seem to be in a rush, so they continued talking. When Suzy called her husband a second time, fifteen minutes later, Ervin went home. Later that night, Suzy called Fate and said, "I know what you're doing. You want to drag him back into a life of sin, Lafayette Jolly."

"Syl, I asked Suzy if she was crazy. She thinks that just because Ervin had some heroin-high dealings with men in his past life, he might want that again and that I'll be the first one he'll come to for it."

"Oh, right," Syl said. She'd forgotten about Ervin's former heroin addiction and his testimonies about some of the things he did during that period. To him, they were all sins he hoped God would forgive. "Ervin isn't interested in men that way. Even I know that. He was strung out. Suzy needs to believe him. The rest of us do."

"Exactly," Fate said.

Gloryanne Gerrard, who was at least fifteen feet in front of Syl and Fate, paused and turned around. When they got closer to her, she said, "I thought I was the only one who saw that snub you got from the Whites."

"Oh God," Syl said, mortified. "You heard me?"

"You know the breeze carries sound in the woods," Gloryanne said. "And don't worry about Suzy. Lord, I wish Ervin never told any of us about his *sins.*"

Gloryanne was an upstate native, born and raised, and thought less of people who'd moved to the area from New York City. It didn't matter to her how long they had lived upstate or how much of themselves they gave to the community. "I thought everything was okay between you and the Whites. Didn't they visit your house for about eleven minutes on the day of Mrs. Talbot's little party?"

There's always someone watching. Jesus Christ, Syl thought.

"Eleven minutes is oddly specific, Gloryanne," Fate said. "Did you write down the coordinates for where they stood on Syl's porch? Damn."

Gloryanne rolled her eyes and sighed. "Am I right, Syl?"

"Yeah, you're about right."

"Well," Fate chimed back in. "If they're mad at anyone, it's probably me. Maybe they don't like that you and I came together, Syl."

"You *did* do a number on them during that trial," Gloryanne said to Fate.

"I like that bracelet," Fate shot back sarcastically. "Darren still doing penance for his *own* sins?"

"Thanks," Gloryanne said. "And yes, he is." She and Fate laughed and high-fived each other.

"Like you said, Fate, it's probably just them grieving," Syl said, ignoring their banter.

"They were warm with me," Gloryanne said, causing Syl to sigh. "But you're right. For them, today is basically like a funeral for Morgan."

Twenty minutes later and about a half mile into the woods,

James had everyone stop at a clearing where there was a beautiful long bench made of thick, sturdy-looking tree parts.

"This is where he liked to sit and sketch," James announced as they all stood around him and Ella, who sat on the bench. "Could we all join hands for a minute? You know we're not prayin' people, but Ella wants to say a few words."

Ella stood and joined the circle. To Syl, her face looked gaunter than when she'd last seen her. "Thanks, everyone, for coming. It means a lot to us. You all know where James and I were when Morgan passed on. So, you can imagine what we suffered, not being able to attend the service my mother-in-law arranged, and not being able to talk to each other about the profound loss. Those days are just too hard to recount. If you're wondering why James and I aren't drenched in tears today, it's because we're fresh out. Almost literally. But know that we are in great pain." There were hums of understanding in the crowd. "We are even angry today. Angry that our sweet, smart, handsome son is gone forever. And for reasons I intend to get to the bottom of, if it's the last thing I do." More understanding hums. But Syl was unable to contribute to the humming.

What does that mean? Syl wondered. *Do they know something about why Morgan was in D.C.?* Syl was also holding back what she knew would be a loud sob. She didn't want to draw attention from Ella. No matter how she felt about it, Ella was the person Morgan had called "Mom."

"I love you, Morgan, my sweet boy," Ella said up into the trees. "Mother will handle this. You'd better believe it."

As the group walked back down the trail, Syl heard Mrs. Talbot ask the Whites if they'd contacted lawyers in the D.C. area yet to learn how the class-action suit was going. To that Ella said, "Yes, we've had a few calls. Thank you."

Once the group arrived back in the parking lot and everyone was wishing everyone else a nice day, Syl sidled up to James, Ella, and Hoke. James and Ella looked eager to get back to their car but were being polite and listening to whatever Hoke was talking about. They also seemed to think they'd turn to stone if they looked at her.

"What's happenin', Syl?" Hoke asked.

"I'm fine. What do you three have planned for the rest of this beautiful day?" Syl asked.

Hoke started to list the outdoor chores he needed to do, adding that he'd have his children help. James cut him short.

"Hoke, it was nice talkin' to you, man. We've gotta get goin'. Syl, did your kids make it safely down to Atlanta?"

"Yes, they did, thanks," Syl said, thinking it was nice of him to ask.

"That's too bad," James replied.

"I'm sorry?" Syl said, perplexed.

"That they couldn't be here today," James added. "But some other time."

"Did they *find* Reggie easily when they arrived in Atlanta?" Ella asked, her arms folded across her chest.

"*Find* him?" Hoke frowned.

Syl was glad he had said it. It confirmed how odd the question was. *Jesus Christ. What do they know?*

Syl steadied herself and kept her composure. There was a chance she was being paranoid—given her petty theft at their house. She still felt awful for stealing the pages from the journal. But the Whites were grieving, she reminded herself again. Their moods and Ella's question might have nothing to do with her at all.

"Yes," she replied. "Reggie picked them up from the station."

"Well, good for them," James said. Syl thought she heard a

hint of sarcasm, but she brushed it off again as her own anxiety. *They would've cursed me high and low if they knew what I told Morgan.*

"Oh, excuse me, people," Hoke said. "I've gotta ask Curt something before he leaves." He wished them a nice day and hurried off.

"Ella, James," Syl said, "if you two need anything, don't hes—"

"I'm tired, James," Ella cut in. "Let's go."

James narrowed his eyes at Syl just enough to make her flinch. "You have a good day, Syl," he said with a smirk, and he followed his wife to their car.

En route to Fervent, Syl told Fate about James's and Ella's odd comments.

"Syl, you're letting your guilt over stealing those pages get to you. There's nothing to worry about."

"I have a feeling in my stomach that they know something, Fate."

"There's no way they know Morgan learned the secret from *you,* then held a memorial service with you there and me tagging along. With the tempers they have, they would've raised all kinds of hell. Come on, Syl. If I've been able to stop worrying so much that they'll punish me for the testimony, I know you can relax. Ask God to forgive you for going in that box and backpack and let's move on. I really believe everything's alright. You got the pages that would've had any mention of us telling him the secret. It's fine."

CHAPTER THIRTEEN

Anyone who has ever smelled a toy fresh out of its box or plastic container knows the smell of Aco, Inc. The parts to all those toys aren't made from scratch at Aco, but its employees do the assembly and packaging for many of the things one might see on the shelves at Toys "R" Us, Kmart, Roses, and the like.

The owners of Aco were known for treating their employees exceptionally well. Could they pay their staff an extra fifty cents per hour? They could, but the people working at Aco were all making more than the minimum wage, which was uncommon. At least half the women had worked at Elm's Feed, and they didn't have much nice to say about their former employer or its management.

Aco's owners were honest people who cared about their staff. So it wasn't a huge surprise to Syl when, on the Monday after the memorial walk for Morgan, she saw James in Aco's parking lot at a quarter to eight o'clock, lunch box and coffee thermos in his hands, strutting toward the employee entrance.

"I should've known he'd be back," she whispered inside her car. "Damn." James was wearing a pair of faded denims and a yellow T-shirt with the words "Pink Floyd" printed on it. Syl didn't know what that meant. His face was clean-shaven. Had he put on a suit, he might have looked as though he was going for an interview at a bank.

"Don't switch on *any* machines yet, folks! Don't switch on *any* machines!" Syl's supervisor, Brian, shouted cheerfully down the hall as Syl waited in line to punch her time card. "Mr. and Mrs. Acosh would like to make an announcement to us *allll*!" He held the "all" out for four counts. Brian, a large white man with a wide mane of frizzy brown hair, did his best to keep morale up. He was always kind and playful, but Syl thought he was laying it on too thick for so early in the week. She knew the Acoshes' announcement would be about James's return.

"What's the announcement, Brian?" someone shouted back. "Are we getting stock in the company?" Laughter filled the hallway.

"Someday, but not today, Orville," Brian said, unable to hold in his laugh. "Today's announcement is about community and the family we're all a part of here at Aco. I know some of you must've already seen a certain *someone* here who we haven't seen in a long time. It's a happy day, people!"

Once the whole staff was in the production room, the Acoshes walked in, followed by James, who had his hands clasped in front of himself. Mrs. Britney Acosh was full of cheer and enthusiasm. It was like a scene out of that movie Syl and Fate had seen together a few years ago, about factory workers unionizing. *Was it* Norma Jean, Norma Rae*?* Syl couldn't remember the title precisely.

"We are so very excited to welcome James White back today," Mrs. Acosh shouted, accustomed to having to compete with the loud machines. Syl heard a man standing behind her whisper that he'd be looking for a new job. "One of our own, and his dear wife, has been to hell and back." Many people in the crowd nodded in agreement. "I don't need to list for *any* of you what I mean by that, because we all know what they've endured and lost in the past couple of years. But they persevered!"

There was clapping. Then Travis Acosh spoke.

"We know we don't *really* have to say this, because you wouldn't even still be working here if you didn't have a sense of family and community in your heart. All the gushiness would have run you off a long time ago," he said, gesturing toward everyone in the room. "Brit and I know all of you will respect James's privacy and his will to move forward, make a living, and have peace, just like the rest of us. But we do ask that, from this moment forward, you keep all your questions and opinions about what James has endured to your*selves.* At the *very* least, don't talk about it here at Aco. If James wants to share, he will when he's ready."

There was noticeably less clapping.

"Travis and I always, *always* believed the authorities had it all wrong. We *knew* it! And we are so happy today has come."

As the couple continued speaking, Syl stopped listening. Despite believing that Fate was right about not needing to worry that she'd been found out, something in the way James and Ella had behaved toward her in Cairo still unnerved her. Today, James looked solemn. No anger on his face whatsoever. He was a bit fidgety. Rocking slightly. Forward and back, just as he'd done on the day he and Ella visited Syl's house. Heels to toes. Heels to toes. All the brawn didn't match how humbled he looked in front of her.

Maybe today he won't be so strange with me, Syl thought.

Over the next week, James was hard to read, staying focused on his work. He greeted Syl a couple of times, but he seemed to have no interest in stopping to have a conversation with her. Given that they hadn't been close friends before Hope's murder, she didn't let that bother her. *But he and Ella thanked me for being so kind to Morgan while they were away. He ought to at least have weather talk with me, right?*

Syl observed him making small talk at lunchtime with some of the guys. Most of the men ate together at one long table in the large break room, and the women mostly took up the other three long tables. That wasn't the extent of their self-segregation. One end of the men's table was all white. All of the other men sat at the other end. The same was true at the women's tables.

One day at lunchtime—it was James's first full week back—he sat at the women's table, at the end where the Black women sat. Everyone who noticed him approaching stopped what they were saying in mid-sentence. He set his lunch box and thermos across from Syl. Selena Barney usually sat in that spot, so her sister Emma turned to James and stared.

"Now, James White, we glad to have you back, but you know we funny about our seats," Emma joked. "Go on and get out of Lena's seat before she comes making a fuss."

"I want to sit here today," James replied with a big smile. "I missed yous. I'll get myself another chair when Selena comes. How's that?" He gave Emma a loud kiss on her cheek, causing everyone to laugh nervously or whistle. Then he went about saying hello to everyone one at that end of the table, one by one. Except Syl.

"You don't see your neighbor Syl sitting right in front of you?" Emma asked him, stirring her bowl of what appeared to be ground beef and succotash, her bangles making music. Now that she was no longer working on the assembly line, she could wear them.

"I'm sorry, Emma," he said. "I thought I got everybody. Hi, Syl." He did not look at her.

"Hi, James," Syl said.

"Anyway, I wanna know how yous are doing," he said, looking from woman to woman.

After asking a few of the women how their families were, he said, "Now, girls, listen up, listen up. I have a question, and I'm gonna need at least, I don't know, two to three opinions." The women continued eating, stirring their food and glancing up at him, waiting. "On top of us having to deal with all the legal stuff around our own cases, and the suit for Morgan's passing, Ella and me found out that while we were locked up, we got betrayed. We're pretty damn mad about it. Mad and hurt. Especially Ella, because I didn't even know about the situation. But either way, we're both fuckin' mad about it. What would you do about it?"

Syl set her fork down.

"There's nothing to do about it," Hortense said, her Jamaican accent demanding everyone's attention. "The betrayal already happened. You should ask what we did to *survive* the hurt. We all, every *one* of us, has probably been betrayed at a high cost. Haven't we, girls?"

Almost every woman within earshot hummed in agreement.

"How serious of a betrayal is it?" Hortense's daughter, Crystal, asked. "If the betrayal didn't cause your death or for you to lose everything you have, maybe it's not the end of the world? You just don't deal with the person ever again."

James seemed to ponder the question for a moment.

"Me and Ella think it caused us to lose something pretty damn special. The problem can't be fixed."

Hortense clicked her tongue. "You riddling too much. Tell the person they hurt you and move on. Like I said, we all been betrayed. Cryssy said it right. Now you know you can't trust the person and you move on with life. You and Ella come through a whole lot and you're strong. You'll be alright. Trust in God."

James unwrapped his sandwich vigorously. He turned the color of a Red Delicious apple.

"Thank yous for listenin'," he said. He repacked his lunch box and left the break room.

"Anybody know what in the world he's talking about?" Emma asked. "That sure as hell isn't the conversation I expected from him."

"How's his wife doing, Syl?" Crystal asked. "You think she'll go back to work soon?"

Syl was terrified that James had been referring to her telling the secret. It took all the strength she had to keep her legs still under the table. And the smell and sight of the food at the table made her stomach lurch.

"Syl?"

"I don't know," Syl replied. Her heart was beating faster by the second, and her face felt hot. "I'll be right back." She walked briskly to a single-occupancy bathroom and waited for the retch that wouldn't come. It was a familiar feeling. She'd had it when she'd learned of Reginald's affair. A panic attack, her doctor later told her.

After lunch, Hortense came to check on Syl in the warehouse.

"Feeling okay? Looked like you felt sick or something."

"Yeah, I'm alright. It's just that with James being back, I think about Morgan and what he meant to me and my kids so much more. It's just hard. So I know James and Ella are having it rough."

"Well, I'm sure you and the other mothers in your neighborhood will check in on her," Hortense said. "She may not ask you all for company, but she needs it. James, too."

"We'll be there for them when they're ready for us," Syl said, nodding. Before she knew it, tears were running down her cheeks. Hortense stood next to Syl and started rubbing her back.

"It's okay, hon," Hortense said.

"I'm sorry," Syl said. "Don't pay me any attention."

Syl considered, for a quarter of a second, confessing to Hortense, right then and there, that she had told Morgan that his birth parents were alive and possibly in D.C. She would tell Hortense that she had done it because Morgan, a young Black man, needed to know that his Black birth parents might, at last, be able to offer him something special. But telling Hortense, or anyone, felt too risky.

"You don't have anything to apologize for," Hortense said. "No crime in grieving a friend."

They stood without speaking for a minute while Syl wiped her tears and blew her nose into a tissue Hortense had pulled from her smock pocket.

"Oh," Hortense said. "How's that book you've been reading at lunch? I noticed you didn't have it today." Syl had forgotten how uncomfortable Hortense could be with awkward silences.

"I like it. The book club meeting is this evening, but I don't think I'll go." The word around Fervent was that Peaches had chosen it as a weed-out book, since the book club was new.

"I think you should go," Hortense said. "Take your mind off work and all."

CHAPTER FOURTEEN

Just minutes after the seven book club members sat down at Peaches's dining room table, the doorbell rang. Syl heard Peaches say, "Glad you made it," and Ella came around the corner, a copy of *Song of Solomon* in hand. Syl and Fate, sitting side by side, glanced at each other. Fate exhaled slowly.

"Hi, everyone. Sorry I'm late," Ella said, making brief eye contact with everyone. "I lost track of time reading. I *just* finished it."

"It's no problem," Peaches said, as she unfolded another one of those uncomfortable metal chairs for Ella to sit on. "We're just settling down to start. There's ice water, and orange juice, and cold canned colas on the kitchen counter, if you want. Help yourself. Don't be shy."

"Thanks, Peaches, for inviting me. I appreciate it," Ella said.

As Peaches thanked everyone for supporting her first try at starting a book club, and talked about what the next book would be, Syl let her eyes roam around the table, taking an inventory of who was likely to continue with the club and who, like her, would be an off-and-on member. She also thought about what she might say to Ella at the end of the meeting. Given how aggressively Ella had ignored her in recent days, she wondered if the Whites had somehow come to learn that Morgan knew the truth. But Syl, once again, shooed that possibility away. She couldn't imagine the Whites knowing and not saying anything to her about it.

Syl saw Suzy John, once again, staring at Fate in a peculiar, distrusting manner. When she and Suzy met eyes, Syl observed that Suzy worked hard not to look back at Fate. And true to form, she began fingering the cross that dangled from her necklace.

"Now," Peaches said. "Fate, will you get us started?"

"After being up in front of my summer school kids all day, and after all the talking I did at today's faculty meeting, I thought I'd get to sit back and relax at *this* one."

"Yes, it was *The Fate Jolly Show* at today's faculty and staff meeting," Ella chimed in, adding a sigh of her own. There was some nervous laughter at the table. "I'm sure you're exhausted from all that, so I can start the conversation here."

"*The Fate Jolly Show*?" he asked. Fate set his book on the table, and Syl knew he was about to say more. "I was merely voicing concerns and—"

"Yes, Fate, we know," Ella cut in without even looking in Fate and Syl's direction.

Ella had never been this way with Fate in front of a group of people. Given what had happened at Aco, Syl was beginning to wonder if James and Ella planned to start harassing the two of them.

Syl tapped Fate on the thigh. He knew what it meant and said nothing more.

"What's something you loved about the novel, Ella?" Peaches asked, attempting to redirect the conversation.

"Let me first say, Peaches, that I *loved* this book," Ella began. "I'm more of a biographies and *auto*biographies kind of person, but I learned a lot from this novel." She went on to say that she was especially taken by the relationship between Milkman and

Guitar. "It gave me a lot of insight into the bonds Black men can have with one another. That's something my son didn't get to have."

Morgan and RJ were very good friends, Ella, Syl thought.

"Macon Senior was *already* a hard character to like," Ella continued, "but it really pissed me off that he decided to tell Milkman unflattering things about Ruth. Milkman simply didn't need to hear it. Macon's intent was to destroy the relationship between a mother and her child. That was an old secret that could've remained buried. It didn't do Milkman a *bit* of good to know it. Macon's decision to share it was plain evil. All it did was hurt his son. I'm curious to know if anyone felt similar." Ella's gaze moved around the table, landed on Syl for a few seconds, and continued its rounds.

What the fuck? Jesus. Maybe Morgan did tell someone here in Fervent that I'd told him the secret, Syl thought. *Stay calm.*

"Well," Margaret England said, setting her book on the table in front of her. "I certainly wouldn't want my children to hear something strange like that about me. But it seemed to me that Macon Senior's purpose for telling the story was to explain *why* he had hard feelings toward Ruth, and he felt like Milkman was old enough to hear it."

"I understand, Margaret," Ella said. "But just because Morgan was *old* enough to hear it didn't mean he *needed* to hear it. What use—"

"Milkman," Belinda Fleming cut in.

"What?" Ella asked. She looked like she wanted to bite Belinda's face off.

"*Milkman* is the character's name. You called him—"

"We know what you meant to say, Ella," Peaches said. "What were you saying?"

"Oh," Ella said. She looked down at the book. "Yes, I meant

to say *Milkman.* Ummm, to add insult to injury, Macon didn't even tell the story *truthfully.* Ruth was *not* in bed naked with her dying father."

"Macon's lies," Margaret England chimed in. "Now, *that's* what made it evil. I didn't have a problem with him telling Milkman about Ruth and her father's strange rapport. The young man needed to know his mom was more than just a mother and wife. It made him see her as a whole person."

Syl, still wondering who Morgan might have told, felt vindicated by the debate. She flipped through the book's pages quietly, not wanting to make eye contact with Ella.

Fate raised a finger, and Peaches called on him.

"In that vein," Fate began, with a hint of orneriness in his voice that Syl wished he would refrain from, "I think we should discuss Milkman's learning, from a *friend,* that he had an aunt and two cousins, right there in the same city, who he'd never met."

God, help me, Syl thought, wondering why in hell Fate would take it there. It was too much. Too close to home. She tapped his foot with her own. He seemed to think it was just an accident.

"Say more," Peaches said, suddenly sounding like teacher of the year. Fate slid to the end of his chair.

"Milkman's meeting Pilate, Reba, and Hagar introduced him to a whole new world, really," Fate said. "Couldn't you all feel how excited he was to know them?"

"Time is flying," Syl said. "Can we talk about Pilate not having a navel?"

"We'll get there," Peaches said.

Ella set her book in her lap and said, "Yes, Fate. Introduced him to a whole new world, and Hagar eventually tried to kill him. You fucking idiot!"

Belinda gasped. Suzy made the sign of the cross, grabbed her pocketbook from the floor, and said, "I knew this book club would cause problems. This novel is *full* of devilment, and I wish I hadn't read it. I'm leaving. Some of *you* are full of devilment, too." She looked straight at Fate.

"Oh, sit down, Suzy," Nel Somers said, pulling Suzy back down to her chair. "You need to read and discuss something other than the Bible sometimes. Sit back down and listen."

Just then, Lorraine Mackey came in smelling of the cigarette she had obviously just finished. A faint stream of smoke was still coming from her nose.

"Sorry I'm late, girls," she said. And when she saw Fate: "And boy."

"Turn right back around, Lorraine," Suzy said to her. "They're in here arguing and cursing already. Let's go."

Lorraine ignored her. "I was just on the phone with my niece. She got wind there's another crazy white man threatening to kill all us Blacks, here in the Hudson Valley," she said.

"Say what?" Suzy said.

"Actually, this one says he'll kill anybody who ain't white, they're saying," Lorraine added before coughing. "Said he wants the Hudson Valley to be all white again. Turns out, his *parents* aren't even old enough to remember when it was hardly none of us up here. So, I don't know what he's talking about."

"Oh yes," Peaches said. "A lady at the dry cleaner's this morning said she heard rumblings about this, too. Another so-called fan or disciple of Josey's."

"And neither of you thought to call around and tell us until now?" Suzy scolded.

For once, Syl was in agreement with Suzy John. Why weren't her neighbors more alarmed? Even Fate seemed at ease.

"They're saying the guy isn't right in the head," Lorraine clarified, then coughed. "You know, didn't make it past sixth grade.

Mind don't work like ours do. You know what I mean. He's just making noise, and people happened to hear him. He ain't smart enough to do what he says he will."

"Well, where *is* this person?" Suzy asked.

From what Lorraine had gathered, the man's name was Sullivan Gray. He'd been shouting at a McDonald's in Lake Pleasant, New York, that he and his family wanted to go back to where their people had once owned lots of lands and a big farm. Why he thought Black people were a problem, Lorraine wasn't sure.

"I doubt it's Black people who own all that land now," she said. "My niece said he was screaming that he wanted to make America all white again, that he'd start in his hometown of Kingston and its surrounding towns. Said he wants to cleanse the area of us, honey," Lorraine said, laughing and coughing at once. "He's not right in the head, girls. He's missing at the moment, but we don't need to worry about him. He just needs to be in one of those psych wards or someplace."

"Missing? And you're saying we don't need to worry? Jesus Christ," Suzy said. "We should all be home locking ourselves in and—"

"Hold your horses," Fate said. "Gray isn't coming around here to bother anyone. He's probably already forgotten he said any of it, if he's got mental problems."

"I know you think you know everything, Lafayette," Suzy shot back. "But you don't know that man's mind."

"Suzy, you heard what I just said," Lorraine chimed back in. "Nothing to worry over. Whoever takes care of him will make sure he doesn't do anything crazy—well, unless they're crazy, too."

"They may be," Fate said. "But think of all the upstate rednecks who've burned crosses in front of churches, much like it was often done in the South. None of them has tried to kill *all* Black people. If this Sullivan guy is serious, why's he waiting?"

Syl sat quietly, trying to decide how worried to be. The whole thing reminded her of an awful incident that had occurred back in Elizabeth City, North Carolina. It was 1952. Syl was just ten years old when she and her mother were awakened in the middle of the night by a glass bottle crashing through their living room window. Teenagers, the children of Ku Klux Klan members, were the culprits. They went from house to house, breaking windows and shouting, "Wake up, niggers!" Though Syl's mother, Agnes, ordered her to get into their one closet, Syl first peeped out a bedroom window and saw the white teenagers who were gleefully wreaking havoc on their homes and senses of safety. It amazed Syl that people so close to her age could be so scary.

Fate and Lorraine were making sense, and no one could argue with them—except Suzy John.

"You all need to pray for God's help, and for some common sense. I'm getting my family and going to Philly until we know this person is somewhere being supervised."

"Suzy, calm down," Nel said.

"Calm *down*?" Suzy shouted. Her eyes bulged as though she wanted to scream. "What is the matter with—" She looked around the room at each face. "You all are taking this *way* too lightly."

Syl was half inclined to agree with Suzy, but kept quiet and listened. Ella, she noticed, also appeared to be weighing how concerned they should all be.

"As Fate just said, think of all the times we've been in so-called danger of someone who has escaped from one of the nearby prisons, for example," Peaches said. "And some of them were convicted murderers, born and raised right here in Saugerties."

"Gray isn't coming from a prison," Suzy said.

"I know, but my point is that they always run away from where they're expected to be. Harry Winfrey, the Banks guy, there've been so many. And they always get caught far from us."

"Exactly," Fate said. "Trust me, girls. Gray is no *true* disciple of Josey's. Just an unwell person who's chosen a terrible hero."

"I agree," Ella said. Everyone looked at her. It was the first time she'd spoken since calling Fate a fucking idiot. "We shouldn't overthink this. It doesn't sound like this guy has the—the *tools* to do what he yelled out in Lake Pleasant."

"It's nice to see you two agree on *something*," Nel said.

"Ladies and gentleman," Peaches said, turning to face everyone, "tell you what. We're all distracted now." She glared at Lorraine playfully. "Why don't we reschedule the discussion of *Song of Solomon*?" Everyone seemed to agree with that plan and started gathering whatever they'd brought with them. "In the meantime, let's all be careful."

"Before we go, I think we should join hands and pray. God and *only* God can—"

"Not this time, Suzy," Peaches said.

Suzy squared her shoulders and said, "Suit yourselves," and she headed for the door.

As the others were gathering their things, Nel said, "Ella, I know you're going through a lot, but I think you owe Lafayette an apology for the way you spoke to him. It was uncalled-for."

"Nel," Fate said, shaking his head.

"No, no," Nel said. "I'm simply stating what everyone here is thinking. Ella was wrong. I think an apology is in order."

"You're right," Ella said. She turned to face Fate and said, "The way I spoke to you was unacceptable. I am sorry. If one of my goals is to rebuild some trust around here, showing kindness is probably where I should start. I am sorry, Fate."

Fate simply nodded. Syl was standing close enough to nudge him with her elbow. He looked over at her with a frown. Then he turned back to Ella and said, "Thank you."

Syl and Ella made brief eye contact. Ella clenched her jaw and turned to leave.

Outside, Syl walked to the edge of Peaches's yard with Fate.

"Fate," Syl whispered. "Ella knows. She has to."

"Knows what? That we told Morgan the secret?"

She reminded him of what Ella had said about Milkman almost being killed by Hagar.

"Oh shit," he said, looking toward the Whites' house. "I was so pissed at her for what she said about me at today's faculty-staff meeting, I didn't put it together."

"I don't know what to do." They walked toward Syl's house, not speaking for about a minute.

"You know, Syl," Fate said. "Let's say they found out somehow and that's the reason they've been so curt with the two of us. Let's just let them. If it makes them feel better, let's let them have their little digs, and not say hello to us at work. Time'll heal their grief and anger. They've done a year and a half in prison and neither of them wants anyone calling the police on them for anything. If being a couple of assholes is how they want to get back at us, we can handle that for a while."

"I don't want to handle it at all."

"Me neither," Fate said. "But they're not beating us up like they did the Hopes."

Once they arrived at the edge of Syl's driveway, Fate turned to her and said, "I think we're okay, Syl. Really, I do."

She hoped he was right.

CHAPTER FIFTEEN

A full day passed and the authorities in Lake Pleasant hadn't located Sullivan Gray. His mother, when interviewed on the air by a local news reporter, said her son lived in a fantasy world and that he was probably there in Lake Pleasant, where they had been living for sixteen years.

Syl didn't know whether she should be more worried about the Whites likely knowing she'd told Morgan the secret or Gray being on the loose.

"He's not gone far. I promise you," Lindsey Gray said to the reporter. Syl watched and bit her nails. "And he wouldn't hurt a bug."

"How did your son come to idolize Christopher Josey?" the reporter asked.

"I don't know," she said. "Probably just listening to the guys he works with and that kind of thing. We don't have anything against Blacks in our house."

The Lake Pleasant authorities notified Saugerties's and Kingston's police chiefs of the threats made by Gray, noting that he hadn't been seen in twenty-four hours. There seemed to be no effort on the part of Ulster County authorities to find Gray or warn its vulnerable citizens. Even the people at Aco, Inc., mentioned the threat only in passing, saying they weren't afraid of Gray. While Syl understood Fate, Ella, and Peaches's reasoning for not worrying too much about his threats, she couldn't help but have some fear.

Syl was halfway between her refrigerator and the kitchen counter when she heard Fate's car pass her house. He still hadn't had his muffler repaired. From her kitchen window, she watched him go inside his house with a couple of grocery bags. She waited five minutes before dialing his number.

"It's late," she said. "Why are you just getting in at this ungodly hour?" It was only nine-thirty. "Another half hour and I was going to start getting worried."

"You're not worried now?" he asked. "Never mind. I know you are. About Gray, and about the Whites knowing what we did."

"Gray's mom says he's harmless," Syl said. "I hope she knows her child as well as she thinks she does. Where've you been?"

Fate told her he'd had meetings with the parents of a couple of his summer school students. Then he went to Lowe's for gold spray paint to recoat some of his wall ornaments. After that, he had a drink with a couple of the other teachers who were also teaching summer classes. Then he stopped at the grocery store to get what he needed to bake a carrot cake for Vincent, who was due to arrive early the following morning. Fate talked for so long, giving each detail, that Syl knew he was holding something back.

"Ahh, okay," she said.

"What, Syl?"

"You're talking in circles. Be honest with me, Fate Jolly. Did you see the *other* one tonight?"

"I don't know who you're talking about," he said coyly.

"Fate, come on now," she said. "Someone's going to get hurt."

"Blu and I aren't sleeping together, Syl."

"Maybe not, but you're getting emotional with him. Vincent told you he didn't like it."

"Vincent said he doesn't like Blu. I don't pick and choose who he goes to drinks with. He's not going to tell me who I can hang with."

"Okay," Syl said. She noticed she hadn't put the lemon meringue pie in the refrigerator, so she did so while speaking. "I'm staying out of it. But it was *you* who told me that the gay New York world is small and that cheating is risky. Even riskier now with the illness that's spreading. I heard men in California are getting sick from it and dying quickly."

"Yeah," Fate said. "It's pretty serious. That's why I'm not sleeping with anyone except Vincent nowadays. He and I agreed."

"Good."

"But Vincent isn't social enough to hear anything about who I'm seeing up here, girl. Thanks for your concern, but I promise everything's above water."

"Good." Then, sensing his irritation with the subject, Syl said, "I miss Hoke."

"I can tell. You all in my business. Where is he?"

"He had to go to Connecticut for something," she said. "Anyway, your business is a little more interesting than mine."

"I wish you were right."

"Hey, I think *our* police should take this Gray situation more seriously. Don't you? Even a little?"

"Not really, Syl." Fate repeated, in short, all the reasons he still believed that Gray wasn't a real threat. "I think you wondering if or when Ella and James are going to confront us is also making you nervous about *other* things."

Syl chewed on that for a few seconds and said, "Probably so. I—"

"Oh," he interrupted. "Speaking of the secret: today at work, Ella nodded hello, but she didn't part her lips or speak a word to me."

"You didn't expect more *this* soon, did you?"

"No," he said. "I guess not." He asked Syl how James had been acting at Aco.

"Quiet. He didn't come around us women much today. I did overhear him saying things about—oh, nothing."

"What?"

"I can't remember," Syl lied.

"Did he say something about me?"

"Not you, but—"

"Ohhhh," Fate said. "He and the men are talking about the gay cancer, aren't they?"

Syl didn't reply.

"Well, Syl, it's a scary thing, and people are going to talk about scary things. I already know that some people at the school are wondering if I'm sick. I'm just waiting for someone to come right out and ask." He sighed. "Anyway, James is still mean, but maybe Ella is the redeemable one. I heard she interviewed for a couple of positions at the hospital. I hope she gets *both* of them. I'm sure she could use a change."

"I wish they'd move away. I'm tired of the—"

"Shit!" Fate said. "I'll be damned."

"What's wrong?"

Fate's visit to the grocery store was right before closing time, he said. All the rushing had caused him to pick up two bags of flour instead of one bag of flour and one bag of sugar.

"Oh well. I'll just go back out to Richmont's Petro in a bit and get it. I can't stand buying things there. They charge almost double the grocery store prices."

"You don't need to go back out tonight, Fate. I have sugar. I think."

"Granulated?"

She asked him to hold on while she checked the cupboard, but she never put down the receiver. She had less than a cup of granulated white sugar, she reported, but plenty of brown.

"That's what I have here, too," he said.

"So use that. Don't go back out, Fate. Please. Not tonight. Not with the crazy man possibly in the area. I don't care what his mother says."

"Okay, okay. I'll stay in."

"Thank you," she said, happy that he'd at least agreed to honor that small request where the threat of Gray was concerned. "I won't call you in the morning if I see Vincent's car in the driveway. I'll wait until around one o'clock."

"Two o'clock," Fate said. "We haven't seen each other in five weeks."

"You're a trip," Syl said, feeling relieved. "I love you, Lafayette Jolly."

"Love you, too, girl."

CHAPTER SIXTEEN

The next morning, Syl was awakened by a persistent light tapping at her front door. *It's Ella coming to let me have it, first thing in the morning.* Syl knew that was unlikely, but the thought was involuntary. She looked at the clock on her bedside table and was surprised to see that it was ten after eight. She was usually up every day at six o'clock.

The knocking continued.

"Pause your gossiping and come let me in," the voice said playfully. It was Vincent.

Syl threw on the T-shirt and shorts hanging on the footboard and went to open the door. Even on a Saturday morning, Vincent was dressed as though he were headed to his job at New York University's main library. In Syl's opinion, he had overdressed. Starched blue shirt, creased linen slacks, and shiny brown penny loafers. The part on the right side of his head was barely visible anymore. It had obviously been a while since he'd visited his barber.

"Hey, Vince," she said. "Everything okay?"

"I'm so sorry, Syl," he said, looking confused. "I thought maybe Fate was over here having Saturday morning coffees with you. But I can see I woke you up." He paused, waiting. "Am I right?"

"Yeah, he's not here." She felt a knot of worry forming in the pit of her stomach. She looked to her right, in the direction of Fate's house, and saw that his car was in the driveway, next to Vincent's. "Hold on. Is this a joke?" She put her hands on her hips and chuckled.

"Huh?"

"Fate sent you over here to try and scare me, didn't he?"

Vincent looked at her, perplexed.

"Sullivan Gray."

"Who?"

"The man who's on the loose and—"

"Syl, I don't know what you're talking about," Vincent said. As soon as the words left his lips, Syl's worry returned. Sweat gathered on her forehead and neck, and her breathing got shallow.

"Is your carrot cake on the kitchen counter?"

"What?"

"Carrot cake. Fate said he was making you a cake."

"Oh, yes, um, yes," Vincent mumbled. He said there were two layers of carrot cake still in their pans. "He hasn't put icing on them yet. I assumed he was letting them cool while he came here."

"Pans still warm?"

"I don't know. I didn't feel them." Vincent said he'd put his bag down in the living room, called out to Fate a few times, and then when he'd realized Fate wasn't there, he'd gone straight to Syl's house.

"Maybe he's out walking or something," she said. "He and Mrs. Talbot, probably. I'll call her house, just to see."

Syl opened the door wider and gestured for Vincent to come inside. She told him about Gray and her fretting—despite others not seeming too concerned at all. Then she dialed Mrs. Talbot's number.

"You've been in London, haven't you?" she asked Vincent. "Or was it France?" She remembered Fate saying he'd gone abroad. "When did you get back?"

"London. And ye—yesterday morning," he stammered. "Last night, I mean." Syl noticed he was averting his eyes.

She waited for Mrs. Talbot to answer her phone. Then she realized there was something different about Vincent's face. "Vince, your lip looks swollen. What happened? You get into a li'l bar fight or something?" It was a joke.

"Mmmm," he said, touching it. "I bit it accidentally last night. It's fine. I'll hold some ice to it later."

Mrs. Talbot said she hadn't seen Fate. Peaches sounded like she was mid-dream when she answered the phone. Everyone else Syl called either didn't answer or said they hadn't seen or heard from Fate. Syl could hear concern in her neighbors' voices. Not being able to find Fate had bad timing. Syl was on edge, and Vincent couldn't stop pacing.

"Let's go back over to the house, Vince. In case he's calling from somewhere." She knew that made no sense. Where would Fate have gone without driving, if not on a walk? And at such an early hour?

She called Hoke and asked him to meet her and Vincent at Fate's, and he said he would walk over in a few minutes.

As the three of them approached Fate's front door, she hoped he'd be there and would tell them he had gone walking in the woods. That, she knew, was a fantasy. Fate wouldn't go into the woods in the morning. He did that only after the dew had evaporated, especially since part of his peace involved lying on warm grass.

"Fate," she called after Vincent opened the front door. "Stop fooling with us and come on out." She went into all three bedrooms and opened the closets. When she got to his bathroom, she noticed the rugs were disheveled, and a pair of boxer shorts was on the floor in front of the tub. Some of the things that would usually be on the counter were in the basin. Then Syl saw that the tub was almost full. No steam or condensation on the mirror or window. But what really concerned Syl was what looked like a boot print on the rubbery white side of one of the bathroom rugs.

"Did you come into the bathroom, Vince?" she asked from the doorway. "Before you went to my house, I mean."

"No. Kitchen and bedroom. That's all."

"It looks like he was about to take a bath but changed his mind."

"Yep," Hoke said after peeping into the bathroom. "Maybe he was in a rush to get somewhere. Doesn't he have a brother in New Orleans who's really sick? Maybe he got a cab to the Albany airport and flew to see him."

"I'd be the first one here in Fervent he'd call if he needed a last-minute ride anywhere."

"Will you two just hush for a minute?" Vincent snapped.

Syl and Hoke glanced at each other.

"I'm sorry," Vincent said. "I'm just—I don't know. Overwhelmed and tired." He walked out onto the front porch, drawing in deep breaths and releasing them forcefully.

Syl called the police and told them Fate was missing under strange circumstances, and, after reminding the officer on the desk about Gray's rumored threats, she demanded something be done.

In the ten minutes that followed, Fate's telephone rang and rang. This neighbor, that neighbor, calling to see if he was home. Then, one by one, they started showing up at the house. Hoke and Curt Bainbridge walked into the woods behind Fate's house, just to make sure he wasn't out there. Nel and her husband drove into the streets surrounding the hamlet to see if they might spot him walking around. Suzy, who had rushed over with her husband and boys, seemed both nervous and inconvenienced. She wrung her hands over and over, and Syl had never heard anyone sigh so many times in a five-minute period in her life.

"You can go home, Suzy, if this is too much for you," Syl quipped. "Thought you all were going to Philly or somewhere." Suzy said nothing in return and left the house.

Once Suzy and her family were out of earshot, Mrs. Talbot said, "Someone should've checked the woods and the river park *before* you all called the police." She must have seen the increased worry on Syl's face because she then said, "Sorry, dear. But that's what the officers will say when they arrive and Fate's sitting here talking with us." She walked through his kitchen and to the back door, then returned to the others in the living room. "His shed door is ajar. Just a little, though. Did any of you check there?" Syl shook her head. "We need to check. Fate could've gone in there and fainted or something." She pushed past them, heading for the back door. Vincent followed. "Syl, you stay here to answer the phone," Mrs. Talbot ordered.

Just then, James and Ella tapped on Fate's front door and came in.

"What's going on?" Ella asked. "I see people coming over here and no one's smiling."

Syl didn't want to look at either of the Whites; nor did she want them in Fate's house. But, in a panic, she filled them in.

Ella and James stood just feet away from Syl. Ella's face had softened, her gaze gentle. Syl took note of how genuinely worried she appeared to be, like she might walk up to Syl and hold her sweaty, shaky hands. James's hands were in his pockets. He seemed more interested in looking around Fate's living room. Syl wondered if he was casing the place to later rob it.

Then Syl heard it. A wail she knew she'd never forget. A man's wail. Some of the people standing there in the house gasped. Syl ran toward the back door and out into the backyard. The man's wail came again.

On the bottom step of Fate's back porch, Syl froze as scream after scream came from the shed, accompanied by the perfectly enunciated "No, God! Baby, wake up! Come on, baby. Wake up for me!" The voice didn't belong to Fate. The pleas were coming from Vincent. Hoke and Curt came rushing back from the woods and into the shed. Syl was still unable to move. She would later wonder if she even blinked or swallowed while standing there.

Seconds later, Hoke and Curt came out, practically carrying Vincent against his will. They seemed to be using all their combined strength to keep Vincent from running back into the shed. His hands and shirt were covered in what looked like mostly dried, sticky blood.

"Wake up, Lafayette! Lafayette, please wake up!" Vincent cried out. Syl, finally able to move, stepped back up onto the porch, bumping into Ella. When Hoke's eyes found Syl's, she knew, without having to ask, what the problem was. Hoke didn't need to say a word. His watering eyes and the tightening of his jaw said it all.

Syl bolted toward the shed, but Hoke shouted for her to stop. She got close enough to the entrance to see that Fate was wearing the white terry-cloth robe she'd gotten him as a Christmas gift the year before.

Syl dropped to her knees and felt the invisible stone of loss lodge itself in her throat. Mrs. Talbot ran to her and knelt beside her. Syl could see Fate's feet, unmoving. His legs were as still as tree trunks. Then Syl wailed her best friend's name over and over again.

CHAPTER SEVENTEEN

Syl couldn't remember the ambulance coming to collect Fate's body. She was crying on his couch, surrounded by neighbors. Mrs. Talbot sat next to her, rocking back and forward with her, handing her fresh tissues every few minutes, holding the small trash bin in front of Syl each time she sounded as if she might be sick. Syl had lost people to long-term illnesses, but no one had ever been taken from her by the hands of another human being. This was a different type of loss entirely.

Thank God my kids aren't here, she thought. She would call them later.

A half hour later, en route back to their houses, Mrs. Talbot said, "Sweetheart, you can't stay home alone. Not with how you're feeling and a killer on the loose. Besides, you're the only Black person in Fervent who'd be home alone. I know anyone here would be glad to have you, and it's just me at my house, as you know." She opened the light jacket she was wearing to protect herself from the cool morning air. "Look at me, dear," she said.

Hoke, standing on the other side of Syl, glanced at Mrs. Talbot's waist and said, "That'll do it."

A gun in a holster hung from Mrs. Talbot's belt. Fate had joked once or twice, after seeing the Talbots having arguments in the produce section at the grocery store, "Mr. Talbot's going to mess around and get shot if he challenges another thing she puts in that cart." Syl had never imagined that Mrs. Talbot actually owned a gun.

"She's right, Syl," Hoke said. "This man is crazy, and he's keeping tokens."

"Tokens?" Syl said.

"He ripped off one of the sleeves. One of the robe sleeves."

Syl put her hands over her face and said, "Why didn't we take the rumors about Gray more seriously, y'all? Why?"

"Dearest, there's nothing we can do about that now, except stay safe and together," Mrs. Talbot said. "Even if Fate had died some other way, you being alone tonight, after losing your best friend, wouldn't be good. I won't have it. I just won't." She rubbed Syl's back. "They'll catch Gray really soon. Mark my words. If he's not too bright, he'll make a huge mistake before long."

"I'll stay in Fate's house with Vince," Syl said. She knew that made no sense the moment she uttered it. Vincent probably wouldn't want to stay in the house himself.

"Nah," Hoke said.

"Vince is in no shape to look out for even himself," Mrs. Talbot said. "If he leaves the police station, I doubt he'll return to the house. But you'd better believe they'll look into where he was last night and this morning—even with it being all but obvious Gray did this. If Vincent doesn't have an alibi, they're not letting him leave that station."

Mrs. Talbot was right about that. She had ears all over Ulster County, including at some of the local police stations. Men gossiped just as much as anyone else, she often said. Syl would later learn from Mrs. Talbot that after being held at the police station for hours, Vincent had called a nearby friend to come and pick him up. Syl hadn't been aware that he had other close friends in the area.

"I don't want to be a burden. But yes, ma'am, I'll stay with you."

"Damn right, you will," Mrs. Talbot said, squeezing Syl's hand. "We'll get through this."

Syl, Hoke, and Mrs. Talbot first went to Syl's house so she could throw a few items into a bag to take with her: a toothbrush, a pair of shorts, a T-shirt, and some underwear. Syl figured she must have lost a cup of tears in the time it took her to toss those things into the small suitcase. She kept remembering the look in Hoke's eyes as he'd told her the news of Fate's murder. There was a small part of Syl that was furious with Hoke for not letting her run to Fate to try to shake him alive.

At Mrs. Talbot's house, Syl was escorted to the guest room and advised to lie down. Mrs. Talbot turned on a box fan in the corner of the room.

"I'll go make some tea."

"Do you have any coffee, Mrs. Talbot?"

"I sure do. Cream or sugar?"

"Black, please. Thank you."

"I'll turn the air conditioner on in another hour or so, when it gets warmer outside. But you let me know if you get hot before then," she said.

"The fan is fine. Thanks, Mrs. Talbot."

Syl stared at the artwork on Mrs. Talbot's walls and thought of Fate. He could look at a painting for ten seconds and know if it had been mass-produced or if it was an original.

Aside from imagining that Gray could be lurking under someone's parked van or in the woods, hiding up a tree, and being grateful that her children were somewhere safe, Syl found that her every thought was about Fate and the glimpse she had gotten of him lying dead in his shed. Even adjusting the pillow under her head made her think of Fate. One day, long before Syl and

Reggie separated, she and Fate had gone to Kmart together, shopping for bed pillows. It was time for hers to be replaced. They'd gotten so flat that she and Reggie were folding them.

"Sylvia Leigh," Fate said. "If you don't put those cheap pillows back and get a better quality, I'll hit you with your *own* pocketbook."

"I'm not spending five dollars on a pillow when they have some for one dollar, Fate."

"That's exactly why you're having to buy new ones every ninety days. Trust me. If you buy these"—he handed her a much firmer pillow from the bin—"you won't have to replace them for six or eight *months.* I promise you."

"Nope," Syl said playfully. But she threw two of the five-dollar pillows into her shopping cart.

He smiled and said, "Maybe it'll fix that thing with your neck."

"What's wrong with my neck?"

Fate laughed and walked away.

"I'm serious, Fate. What's wrong with my neck?"

Mrs. Talbot came back into the room with a tray holding a glass of water, a cup of coffee, and a blueberry muffin on a saucer. She set it on the bedside table.

"I'll be right out in the living room," she said. "I don't imagine you have much of an appetite, but drink some of that water and coffee. Try your best to eat a few bites of the muffin. For lunch I'll make us sandwiches and salad. But for now, lie there and rest."

"I'm not going to be able to sleep, Mrs. Talbot. I—"

"I know, honey. When Grant died, lying still for hours and just thinking about him brought me peace. Well, it made it hurt badly, too, but there was a lot of peace in just letting my mind remember him."

Syl nodded and laid her head back on the pillow. She wished another funny memory would come to mind, but it just wasn't a lucky day.

"My father used to tie my hands behind my back," Fate had told Syl. It was on a late Saturday morning and they were at a McDonald's waiting for GiGi and RJ to finish softball practice. "Then he'd make me stand with my back against the wall."

"What for?" she asked. "You hit someone or something like that?"

"No, ma'am. I didn't hit people. Even if someone hit me first, I didn't fight back. I didn't have it in me in those days." Fate took a sip of his soda. "My father said my arms and wrists were too active, too flappy, that I always had one of my hands dangling from the wrist like girls and women did. So he bound them and put them behind my back so I couldn't give in to whatever mannerisms he hated so much."

"Jesus, Fate." She wanted to slide next to him in the semicircular booth and hug him, but he'd told the story with such nonchalance, she thought her impulse to comfort him might cause annoyance.

"Oh, that's nothing. That's probably the *least* humiliating or uncomfortable thing he did."

"Did your mother step in and stop it?" Syl wished she could rewind and take the question back. It was obvious that his mother either was powerless or condoned the treatment Fate received.

"No. She was half afraid of him, and she half agreed with why he treated me that way."

"I'm so sorry," Syl said, deciding to lean forward to show care.

"Thank you, sweet lady, but *you* didn't do it to me," he said with a nervous chuckle. They sat quietly for a moment. "Tell me something, Syl. If RJ was like me, how would you handle it?"

"Well, I won't lie and say I'd be *thrilled*. People give you all a hard time. But I'd love and protect him even more."

"How do you know you'd still love him just the same?"

"Because I carried that knucklehead inside of me for thirty-seven weeks, nearly had a heart attack when it took the doctors so long to get him crying after he came out, and because I nearly bit a teacher's head off for spanking him without my permission. There's nothing he or GiGi could do or announce that would make me love them any less."

"A lot of parents say that, Syl," he said. "But I believe *you*."

Fate also told Syl about the very first man he ever fell in love with—the man who nearly broke him, causing him to wall his heart up for years.

"Oh, Syl, if you'd asked me about that bastard before I met Vince, I wouldn't have told you a thing about him. But now it's easier to talk about it because I know true love."

"He left one hell of a mark, didn't he?"

Fate explained that his first love—his name was Holland, but he went by Prince—was one of his college classmates. From the moment Fate first laid eyes on Prince, he wanted him, but he believed Prince was off-limits. Fate described Prince as one of the most handsome men he'd seen.

"Are we talking about a pretty type of *handsome*, or—"

"Girl, he was pretty, pretty, all of it. Carried himself like Joe Louis or somebody. Fought like him, too."

"I didn't think you liked the very manly types," Syl said. "And *fought*? Did he do a lot of that?"

"I'll get to that," Fate said, holding up a finger. "I *used* to require that they be masculine. Not so much anymore. Anyway, Prince was smart as a whip and fine as you want, but he had a short fuse, Syl. He could be a bully."

"Fate, don't tell me he hit you."

Fate scoffed. "I wish the story ended differently. The *first* time was just a very hard slap on the face when I'd put on a little bit of lipstick and came out of our bedroom dancing and singing some Billie Holiday. He didn't care much for that."

"Oh, Fate."

"The second time was when he saw me talking to a guy outside the bodega on the corner of our block. He'd been watching from our apartment window."

"You two were living down in the city, right?"

"Right. In the barrio. Prince had a friend whose dad was a super. Helped us get the apartment. This was after we graduated college. Anyway, I went back upstairs to the apartment and he was standing there waiting. 'You sure were doing a lot of smiling while speaking with that turkey down there. Who was he?' I didn't know the guy, Syl. He'd asked me if I knew of a good barber nearby, and I was telling him where I went for haircuts. The guy had said something funny about the cost of things in New York versus where he was from. He was from Arkansas."

"Prince didn't believe you?"

"He believed I didn't know the guy but accused me of *wanting* to know the guy. I told him he was acting stupid and he beat me so bad, I—"

Fate couldn't finish the story, but Syl imagined it was pretty awful.

About an hour after Mrs. Talbot dropped off the water, coffee, and muffin, Syl decided it was time that she go out and join her in the kitchen. Mrs. Talbot had made them both chicken salad sandwiches on pumpernickel bread, and she had quartered them. Syl didn't have the heart to tell her she couldn't stand the taste of pumpernickel.

In the center of the table there was a large wooden bowl of torn iceberg lettuce, cherry tomatoes, and sliced red onion, all tossed together. Thick glass jars half filled with homemade dressings sat at one end of the table. Mrs. Talbot had a small television on the counter. It was tuned to Channel 12.

"I have the news on," Mrs. Talbot said. "When word gets around about what's happened here this morning, I'm sure reporters will be interviewing officers, then making their way here." She turned the volume low and said, "We'll keep our eyes on it."

Mrs. Talbot kept her gun on her hip, mostly, but while they ate—nibbling was all Syl could do—she put it on the table.

"Have you ever fired a gun, Syl?" she asked. This was the third time she'd asked since Syl had come out of the bedroom. Syl figured Mrs. Talbot didn't think she would notice, but after she took a shot of some clear liquor, she also swallowed one of her medications. Syl remembered Mrs. Talbot once saying she took something for allergies during the spring and summer. The medicine and the shot made her a bit more relaxed than Syl was comfortable with—especially since Mrs. Talbot was supposed to be protecting her.

"No," Syl said again. "Held an unloaded gun once, and I kept my finger away from the trigger." With great care and precision, Mrs. Talbot picked the gun up from the table, released the cylinder to show Syl the bullets, closed it, and aimed it at the front door like one of the actresses on *Charlie's Angels.*

"I assure you, sweetheart. I'm not drunk from that one shot of vodka and the allergy pill," she said. "I *also* promise you I can use this gun just as well as any of those policemen who came to Fervent today. If Gray so much as steps on my porch, he'll have a hole in his forehead before he even touches the doorknob. Don't let the manicure and this bouffant fool you." She studied Syl's face for a few moments. "If Grant was still with us, he'd want to sit out *on* the porch and guard us. That was the kind of man he was, as you know. He cared about *all* people. No matter their skin color, religion, any of it. My first husband—" She winced. "I'm embarrassed to say it, but he wouldn't put himself in danger to protect you from Gray."

"He didn't like Black people?"

"I don't think it was so much that he disliked Black people. It was more of a 'none of my business what they do or what happens to them' sort of thing."

"How'd you feel about that, Mrs. Talbot?"

"We were only married a year, if that tells you anything," she said. "I was young, and he was my son's father."

Syl had forgotten that Mrs. Talbot had once had a son. He had been born with a heart abnormality and had slipped away from her when he was a few weeks old. He never even got to leave the hospital.

"Right, right," Syl said. In an effort to distract herself from thinking about Fate's lifeless body, she asked Mrs. Talbot about former Fervent residents—those who had moved out when the first Black family moved in. Mrs. Talbot told Syl about one of the couples, to which Syl remarked, "Sounds like some of them were a handful."

"Yes, they were. I was happy to see them move away. The fact that a Black family buying a house here in Fervent sent them running—" She scoffed and made the gesture of shooing the invisible former neighbors off. "It says all you need to know about them. Sullivan Gray probably comes from that type of stock, though his mother claims otherwise. My husband would be beyond furious about what's happened today. Just absolutely sick with anger." Her voice began to crack, and Syl saw tears well up. "I miss that man so much."

"Yes," Syl said. "I know you do."

After a couple of minutes Mrs. Talbot said, "I'm glad you have someone, Syl." The comment caught Syl off guard. "Hoke's a good fellow. I imagine you two haven't told your children."

"No, ma'am. We haven't. How'd you know about us?"

Mrs. Talbot shrugged and said, "I just happened to be somewhere at the wrong time. A fluke. Don't worry. I haven't told a living soul. Except Grant, of course."

At first, Syl couldn't decide whether or not to say more about her relationship with Hoke. She settled on: "It started at work. After Reggie left, though."

"Oh, you don't have to explain it to me," Mrs. Talbot said, standing to put the gun back in its holster on her belt. "I understand." She walked to the window, peering out. To the right, then the left. "Speaking of Aco, I'm told you and James have had some discord since he's returned to work. He's not speaking to you, I've heard. What's that about? I hadn't planned on mentioning it, but with all we've gone through today, why not talk about it all?"

"I don't think it's very serious," Syl lied. "Just his usual temper."

Mrs. Talbot explained that she played cards with one of the women who worked in the offices at Aco. It was something Syl knew but had forgotten. Why the women in the offices would care who the plant workers did and didn't speak to, Syl didn't understand.

"I also heard Ella snapped at Fate at Peaches's book club meeting."

"Yeah, she did, but she apologized. You know Ella has never been my favorite person, and I know I'm not one of hers. But I'll give her credit: she gave him a nice apology." Syl, without feeling the usual buildup, began to cry, silently, for her best friend. Mrs. Talbot went back to the window and peered out, eyes squinted, though the sun was shining bright.

When Syl's sobs subsided, Mrs. Talbot said, "What had them so fired up toward you two? They've only just got back to town."

Syl rolled the question around in her mind long enough for Mrs. Talbot to say, "Syl, honey. Did you hear me?"

"Yeah," Syl replied, looking at the floor and knowing that she couldn't confess to Mrs. Talbot that she had told Morgan his truth. Since the Whites hadn't confronted her, and since they clearly hadn't told anyone else about the secret she'd told Morgan, Syl thought there was a chance she'd misinterpreted Ella's comments and anger at the book club meeting. *Maybe my guilt made me hear it that way,* she thought. *Or maybe Ella and James understand why I told Morgan, even if they hate that I did.*

"I believe they're upset with Fate and me for getting to spend so much time with Morgan after they went to prison. Especially since I'd told Ella a few times that Morgan needed—"

"To be in a Black household," Mrs. Talbot finished. "I remember now."

Syl knew that Mrs. Talbot straddled the fence on the topic of Black children raised in white homes.

To make the half-truth more convincing, Syl added, "And they hadn't really forgiven Fate for his testimony. It was one of the first things James mentioned when they got back to town."

"That doesn't surprise me. But they'll need to get over Fate's testimony, and their jealousy of you two for being adored by Morgan. Let's also remember that they're grieving. No excuse to be jerks, though. At some point I'll go over and have a word with them. James will listen if I invoke my husband's name. Dear God, my grief for Grant is still as fresh as this morning's eggs. Then Morgan passes, and now we have another person to grieve."

"Fate was my best friend," Syl said, giving in to a new wave of crying. The timing was heaven-sent.

"I know, sweetheart. I know."

They sat quietly until the telephone rang and Mrs. Talbot got up to answer it.

"Well, maybe there *is* a just God," she remarked shortly after saying hello. "That was quick. He must have stolen a vehicle or had someone driving him around. He would've been seen if he were just walking around." She listened to the caller for a minute or so and said, "So, he died?" Silence. "I see. Well, that was compassionate thinking on the man's part." More silence. "Okay, I'll let Syl know right now. Thanks, Peaches. That's one less thing for us all to worry about while trying to mourn."

"Gray's been caught?"

"More than caught. He's dead," Mrs. Talbot said, hanging the banana-yellow receiver back in its cradle on the wall. "He tried to attack a family over in Kingston, but the property owner was ready. Shot him in the thigh so he couldn't run off, but he bled out. The bullet must have hit some main vein or something. May he burn in the depths of hell for what he did to Fate. If it's true that he was mentally challenged, may God forgive him. I can't say that I have that much compassion. Not now, at least."

Syl didn't know a lot about mental illnesses, but she knew that not all people who struggled with them were alike. So she chose not to respond to Mrs. Talbot's comment.

"Was it a Black family he tried to hurt?"

"Peaches didn't say, but I imagine so. I suppose it'll be on the news later."

After Syl and Mrs. Talbot had been sitting in her living room for about an hour, the breaking news report finally came on. The wife of Kingston city councilman Lawrence Downing, the man—a Black man—who had shot Gray, was being interviewed by a reporter.

"We were all in the backyard," Mrs. Downing said. "I was pulling weeds and Lawrence was pushing our daughter on the swing set. In my peripheral vision I saw a person come from around the house, walking quickly toward the swing set, and I almost said,

'Can we help you?,' but when I saw the huge butcher knife in his hand, I screamed, 'Lawrence, stop him!,' and before I knew it, my husband had shot the man in both his legs. We'd heard he was missing and that he might come this way, but we didn't really expect him to. But Lawrence wasn't taking any chances. So, when that man walked into the yard with a knife in his hand, I knew he needed to be stopped, whether it was Gray or not."

"Was it you who called the police, Mrs. Downing?"

"Yes, it was," she said. "After I saw that Gray wasn't able to get up and run anywhere, I hurried inside and called nine-one-one. My daughter was inside by then. She'd run in right after Lawrence fired the shots. Lawrence stood near Gray and kept the gun pointed at him the whole time."

"We're told Gray didn't die right away," the reporter asked. "Is that correct?"

"That's correct," Mrs. Downing said. "I came back outside, stood back, and listened to Lawrence and him exchange words while Gray lay there bleeding and squirming. He cursed us until he drew his last breath. His *very* last breath."

"Are you able to repeat any of what Gray said?"

"I won't," Mrs. Downing said. "Most of it was awful and quite vicious. Lawrence and I heard about the gentleman being found in his shed in Fervent. We hope Gray didn't hurt anyone else before coming here. Lawrence asked him."

"Did Gray respond to that?" the reporter asked. "Do you know if he hurt anyone else before going to your house?"

"Gray's breathing was getting labored, and it was clear he was either about to faint or—"

"But did he say anything else?"

"Yes," Mrs. Downing said. "He started saying something, but with his slurred speech, we couldn't make it out perfectly. To me, it sounded like he said, 'You would've been my worse.'"

CHAPTER EIGHTEEN

On the Monday after Fate's murder, his nieces, Eisa and Renee, visited Syl to ask if he'd been attending church. They couldn't decide whether to give him a religious service or a nonreligious memorial at a community center or some other suitable public place. He had been clear—with Syl, at least—about not wanting his ashes spread in his hometown of St. Louis, but he had left the decision of what type of service to have up to his nieces. They should feel free to do what made them feel comfortable at that time, the document stated.

"He went to church once every few months," Syl told the nieces. "Mostly for the singing."

"That makes sense," Eisa, the younger of the two, said. She couldn't have been older than twenty-five. To Syl, she looked like a brown porcelain doll. Her thick, coarse hair was in a long braid that hung halfway down her back. "He, our momma, and all of them grew up listenin' to gospel and singin' in the choir." Fate had mentioned to Syl that when he was a young boy, he and his siblings were forced into choirs, despite not having the voices for it. His sister was the only one of them who did, he'd said. "What would you do, Miss Sylvia?" Eisa asked. "You knew him better'n we did. Church funeral with a choir, some friends speakin', and a prayer or two. No eulogy from the pastor, maybe?"

"That sounds about right to me," Syl said.

Before leaving Syl's house, Eisa said, "You know, Miss Sylvia, Uncle Fate was a sacrificial lamb."

"How so?" Syl asked, confused.

"Gray had planned to kill a whole bunch of Black folks around here. I heard most people didn't believe he was really comin' because he was mental. But he did, and it put people in nearby towns on watch, which is how he got caught."

"What you sayin', Eis?" Renee said.

"Uncle Fate didn't die in vain. A lot of other lives were saved."

Syl saw the young lady's point, and she agreed.

On the Wednesday after Fate's passing, he was cremated. On Saturday, there was a service at the Pentecostal Holiness church he'd sometimes attended. Renee and Eisa had convinced the pastor to conduct the service the way Fate would have wanted. The church was packed with teachers and their spouses, students and their parents, staff members from the school, bartenders from the two bars where Fate sometimes had an after-work beer, waiters and waitresses from local restaurants, and friends of Fate's from down in New York City. Almost every Fervent resident attended. Syl, Hoke, Mrs. Talbot, and Vincent sat on the fourth pew, behind the family members who'd come to town. Vincent was inconsolable from the moment they pulled up to the church. Syl had been crying for days, so she was grateful to do less weeping at the service.

During the choir's singing of "Near the Cross," Mrs. Talbot went to the bathroom. When she returned, she whispered to Syl, "James is outside. I don't know if he ever came in." Ella was on the pew behind them.

"I don't think he did," Syl said. The pained expression Mrs. Talbot had before stepping out was now one of anger.

"He's behaving like a child," she said. "It wouldn't hurt him to come and sit with his wife and pay his respects." She moved to get up again, but Syl tapped her wrist.

"Let's leave it alone," Syl said. "Maybe he's thinking about Morgan." That could be at least half the reason he hadn't come in. But everyone knew how James felt about Fate.

Mrs. Talbot sighed and said, "Well, I imagine he is, but he can do that in here, next to his wife and with his neighbors." She looked forward and didn't say anything else, but Syl could tell she would have more to say about it later.

"James, come here," Mrs. Talbot said after the service, as she, arm in arm with Syl, descended the church's red-brick stairs. James obeyed, eager to help her down the stairs. "I can get down the steps just fine. What I want to know is why you weren't inside. Would it have been so hard?"

"I, well, Mrs. T." James took a few steps back and slid his hands into his pockets. "I'm just not good with funerals. I—"

"I don't want to hear that," Mrs. Talbot said. She walked down to the landing, stood before him, and looked up into his eyes. Syl stepped to the side. "You were terrible to Fate. Almost unforgivable, if we're being honest." Just then, Ella appeared. Syl wondered if she'd materialized out of thin air. "Both of you were."

"Mrs. Talbot," Ella said. It was clear to Syl that she was fighting hard to keep her cool, but her face was rapidly reddening. "This isn't fair, nor is it the time or place."

A few of the neighbors walking by had stopped to listen. Peaches, Suzy, Nel.

"*You* went in and sat. He should've, too," Mrs. Talbot scolded. "I'm *very* disappointed. Grant would be beside himself today, James. *Morgan* would be, too."

"Yes, he would," Syl chimed in. "Morgan *loved* Fate. He'd become like an uncle or father to him while you two were away. You even *thanked* us for that. I don't understand why—"

"Tread carefully, Syl," Ella said.

And there it was. The ire in Ella's voice said it all. She knew Syl had told Morgan the secret. There was no longer any question about it. But in that moment, minutes after her best friend's funeral, Syl didn't care about Ella's anger.

"It's not our fault you two got yourselves into that Hope shit," Syl said, looking back and forth between the Whites. "Nobody's fault but your own that you got taken away from Morgan. That wasn't my or Fate's fault. We showed the boy *love.*"

Peaches stepped in closer and said, "People, do this another time." But she was ignored.

"When things quiet down," Mrs. Talbot said to the Whites, "I *will* be having a word with the both of you. For now, I'll say this: feel your pain for the son you lost, but stop with all this ill will."

Syl could tell James wanted to punch something. She recognized the flaring of his nostrils. He stormed off toward his car. Ella was biting her bottom lip, and Syl saw beads of sweat rolling down her neck. Then, without saying a word, Ella followed her husband.

In Syl's car, Mrs. Talbot said, "Well, I guess they'll be mad at me now, and *madder* at you. I don't give a damn. They know I'm right. Grant would've given James a piece of his mind today."

"Now do you see why I always thought Morgan should be living somewhere else?"

Mrs. Talbot looked at Syl, but didn't reply.

By the time they arrived at the community center for the repast, Syl felt some guilt about having argued with the Whites at the church. The day was supposed to be about honoring Fate, not fussing with anyone. In truth, she hadn't cared whether or not the Whites attended the service. But when Mrs. Talbot mentioned how Morgan would feel about James's refusal to enter the church for the service, Syl's frustrations with them were ignited. And she knew that sometime soon, Ella would likely call her to discuss the secret.

There had been rumors of a hurricane coming up from the South. The Hudson Valley was expected to get lots of wind and rain. Syl wished that wind and rain would blow and pour and wash her and everyone's recent sorrows away.

CHAPTER NINETEEN

Hurricane Cheyenne didn't take any lives in the Hudson Valley, but it did lots of property damage. The storm left Fervent and a few other Saugerties neighborhoods without electricity or working phone lines for a couple of days. It was the lack of electricity, Syl would later come to believe, that made it possible for her to be knocked out and kidnapped.

The river didn't rise high enough in Fervent to keep its residents from being able to come and go. With Gray dead and no other immediate threat hovering, Syl decided she would be fine at home. She could survive the heat and use her gas stove and charcoal grill to cook the meats that were thawing in the freezer.

She spoke to GiGi and RJ at five o'clock most days. It was one of Reginald's nonnegotiable rules for them to be in his house by five o'clock to help his wife with dinner, so Syl thought she would head out and call them before they got busy. While driving around to find a working pay phone to call the kids, she saw men from the electric company digging holes and climbing poles. As she passed, one of the technicians was leaning on the large utility truck, drinking from a bright orange Igloo thermos. He looked familiar, but Syl couldn't recall why. She slowed down and stopped to ask him when he thought they might get to Fervent.

"We should be on the hamlet by, let's say, eight or nine tomorrow morning," he said. His hair was pulled back in a bushy ponytail, his accent a blend of New York City and Puerto Rico. "If there's no serious damage, we'll have you all's power back on within two to three hours after we get started. Could be sooner, though. Pretty lady like you needs to be in the air-conditioning, yeah?"

"Well, I do look forward to having power," Syl said, offering a slight smile. As handsome as he was, she wasn't in the mood for his flirting. "I work at Aco, but the parking lot flooded, which means there's probably water standing inside, too."

"Probably so," he said. "Sorry for your loss, by the way. Mr. Jolly was a real cool cat."

Then it hit Syl. This man had been at Fate's memorial service. She'd seen him talking to the nieces when it ended.

"I knew you looked familiar. You were at the service last week."

"Yeah," he said. "Mr. Jolly gave me good advice that helped me land this job. Let me tell ya: I'm doing a lot better now than I was before getting it."

"Good. How'd you meet him?"

"Through my ex-lady. A teacher that worked at the high school. We used to invite Mr. Jolly and his boyfriend—or lover or whatever they call it—over for dinner sometimes."

"Oh yes," Syl said. "I remember Fate and Vincent going to another teacher's house for dinner once in a while. Miranda. Or was it Marissa?"

"Yeah. Miranda," he said. "I'll be honest with you, Miss— Oh, what's your name? I'm Javi. Javier Tua."

"Sylvia," she said. "No 'Miss' necessary." She didn't feel he needed to know her full name. What for?

"I'll be honest with you, Sylvia. I didn't care much for Vincent. He talked down to Mr. Jolly, and one of the times they came over to eat with us, I looked out the window and saw what looked like them fussing before they got out of the car. Vincent put his finger to Mr. Jolly's forehead and shoved it. I didn't like that one *bit,* but my lady—my ex—said she knew Mr. Jolly wouldn't be with an asshole. She thought what I saw was them just playing around. But, nah. It didn't look right to me. I could feel that the Vincent guy wasn't nice."

"Well, I'll admit he's not the *warmest* guy," Syl said. "But if it was something serious, Fate would've dropped him. I know that for a fact." That wasn't altogether true. Javier's story made her think of Prince, the fellow Fate had dated during and after college.

"Well, may God rest Mr. Jolly's soul," Javier said, making the sign of the cross. "You have coolers and ice, don't you?"

"I'm going to get ice now. My deep freezer'll be my cooler until you all get the power back on."

"Good, good," he said. "You have a man at home to help you transfer everything from the fridge to the deep freezer?" A larger smile followed his question.

"I do, thank you. And listen: thanks for sharing that with me. About Fate and Vincent, I mean."

"I wasn't trying to start anything. I didn't know either of them too well. But I just didn't like that Vince dude. He had an edge about him that I couldn't shake."

CHAPTER TWENTY

There were nine people in line to use the pay phone at the 7-Eleven, so Syl went to Richmont's Petro to see if the wait might be shorter. She was pleased to find that only three people were waiting there, and she was glad none of them were her neighbors. Syl didn't want to see them gathered together again so soon. The last two times had been somber.

"I feel like we should be there with you, Ma," GiGi said. RJ was also on the line. "But I guess Daddy and Patricia *need* us here now." Reggie had, a couple of days back, fallen and broken his arm and one of his ankles. His wife needed the children's help.

"I'm fine, babies. I'm sure the electricity'll be back on by lunchtime tomorrow. The cabinets are full of canned vegetables *you* two won't eat, and I'll grill the meats."

"How're you holding up?" RJ asked. "Not having Fate around."

"It's been a tough pill to swallow, son, but he's with me. When I get back to Fervent, I'll stop by his house to make sure none of his windows were knocked out by the storm."

"Don't go in there by yourself, Ma," GiGi said. "*Please.*"

"Right," RJ said. "Just go back home. Fate's place is alright. If something's damaged, you can't do anything about it. I don't want you going in there at all."

"Baby, the man who took Fate's life is dead."

"*Still,* though," RJ pleaded. "Something just doesn't sound safe about anybody going in there. See, this is why we want you to go to the city and stay with cousin Trina and them." After Fate's memorial service, her children had advised Syl to take a week away from Fervent. But she wanted the time alone. Her cousin would've only irritated her with the constant vacuuming and shoving plates of food in her face.

"If the power isn't on by five o'clock tomorrow, maybe I'll go to Trina's," she lied. "But that's if the highways up here are cleared. Lots of trees and poles are down. Anyway, you two don't need to worry about me. I'm cool, *jewels.* I'm nifty, *swifties,*" she said in an attempt at hearing them laugh. They did not.

"Ma," GiGi sighed. "Stop it. You're so old."

"Oh!" RJ said. "Speaking of old people, Ma, do you remember growing up with a guy named Clyde McSomething?"

"Yeah," Syl said, remembering the last time she'd seen him. "Clyde Freeman. But his name was changed. Claude McLaughlin. Why're you asking?"

"Well, he's back to *Clyde* now," GiGi said. "And he's the NAACP chapter president for the Atlanta area, or maybe all of Georgia, or something like that."

"He said to tell you hello," RJ said.

RJ and GiGi related that while they were in the mall's food court with Patricia, she had called out to a man who'd passed their table with a woman and three children. The man was Clyde McLaughlin. He, his wife, and their children joined them, and the adults talked for nearly two hours, GiGi said.

"Get outta here," Syl said, wanting more information. Clearly uninterested, the children seemed to have already forgotten about the topic and were starting to speak about something else entirely. Syl interrupted: "Is Clyde's wife Black?"

"Yeah," RJ said. "Why?"

Well, well. Check that out, she mused.

"Nothing. Just asking," Syl replied. Given the lengths the McLaughlins had gone to in order to keep him away from Black people, Syl hadn't expected him to marry a Black woman.

"Why'd his name get changed to Claude?" RJ asked. "Dad and Patricia said they couldn't remember."

Syl thought for a moment about her position on cross-racial adoption, and the fact that her kids had always thought it was far less serious than she did. She wasn't in the mood for a debate. The kids so often won. Reggie and Patricia must not have been in the mood to lose a debate, either.

"I can't remember," she lied. "Glad to hear he's doing well for himself, though. Anyway, I'll walk over to Mrs. Talbot's if I get lonely. She's got plenty of stories to tell me—especially if she takes that allergy pill with a shot of vodka, gin, whatever she drinks." At that, the kids chuckled, which made Syl smile.

As Syl was entering the store after her phone call, James was driving off. To her surprise, he offered a gentlemanly head nod. *Well, I'll be damned,* Syl thought. *Mrs. Talbot must have already given him and Ella a talking-to.* Assuming she was right about the Whites knowing she'd told Morgan about his birth parents, she thought that maybe they'd decided not to confront her and to move on with their lives.

Once Syl got inside Richmont's, Libby Richmont, one of the original owners' daughters, announced that Syl had just missed a neighbor.

"Your famous neighbor," Libby called him.

"Yeah, I saw him," Syl said, still perplexed by the friendly gesture. "Well, I hope they didn't buy up all the ice."

The last thing Syl wanted was to get stuck in a gossipy conversation with Libby Richmont, who spoke too freely with her customers. "Did you all lose power and phone service on your side of the river?" Syl asked.

"Neither. We just have a lot of tree limbs to have chopped and hauled off," she said. "Listen, Syl. I haven't seen you since Fate . . . you know. I just want to offer you my deepest condolences. He was the sweetest thing, and I know just how close you two were. Like sister and brother, I tell people. I'm sorry I couldn't make it to his service. I heard it was lovely."

"It was. And thanks, Libby. I miss him more than I can—"

"Your *famous* neighbor didn't seem to want to hear anything about it."

"Well, after what he and Ella were accused of and did time for, I can't blame them."

"No, I imagine I wouldn't want to talk about a murder, either," Libby said. "Especially *that* type. Still, I was only remarking on how nice Fate was. But Mr. Fights-at-the-Movies just kind of shrugged and scowled."

"That happened today?" Syl asked. "Just before I came in here?"

"Yes."

Given how pleasant James had just seemed, Syl found it odd that he'd been curt with Libby. "Well, he didn't care much for Fate, and the feelings were mutual."

Libby's eyes widened.

Ah shit. Why did I say that? Here we go, Syl thought.

"You know what? I forgot all about what happened during the trial. Your friend's testimony."

"Right," Syl said, stepping backward down the aisle opposite the cash register.

"I bet they never forgave Fate for that. Did they?"

"I don't know," Syl replied. She asked Libby if she had any small bags of charcoal in stock. The family-size pack of ground beef from the deep freezer was thawing and she was eager to get home to make some hamburger patties and grill them. She explained that to Libby.

"Well, I don't imagine you'll be inviting the *famous* ones over for the barbecue?" Libby mused.

"We're not close," Syl said.

"But you and your children were close to their son, I remember. Such a sweet young fellow," Libby said. "For a while, I thought he was one of *yours.* He and your son resembled each other." Syl pretended not to hear that. Morgan looked nothing like Syl or any member of her household. "I'll never forget the day James White shoved Raymond Livesey. It was just over there, in front of the beer cooler, if you can believe it."

"Really?" Syl said, intrigued. "What all happened?"

Libby explained that Raymond, a large man, was standing in the middle of the dead-end aisle that led to the alcohol cooler. He was reading the label of some drink.

"Raymond hadn't heard James walk up behind him, so James said, 'I need to get by you,' and Raymond stepped out of the way. There was plenty of room for James to pass. *Plenty* of space. But James said, 'I said move, goddamn it,' and he pushed Raymond right into the canned-foods shelves. Nearly knocked the whole thing down, but Raymond caught his balance first. When James got to the register, I said, 'Now, that wasn't very nice.' He slammed the money for his beer on the counter, stared me down, and walked out."

"That sounds like James to me," Syl said, thinking about the injury she'd sustained at Aco.

"Yeah," Libby said, ringing up Syl's items. "Anyway, he bought some heavy-duty electrical tape. I figured maybe they're having to tape plastic bags up as temporary window replacements after the storm. You know *me.* I asked him and he said he needed to wrap a few leaky hoses down in their basement and seal something."

"Ah," Syl said. "Honestly, I think it would've been better for them if they'd sealed their house up when they got out of prison, and moved somewhere else."

CHAPTER TWENTY-ONE

While searching through the cabinets above her stove for seasonings, Syl heard a knock at her front door. It was Peaches.

"Has anyone told you the news?" she asked, lifting her Yankees cap and fanning herself with it. It appeared as though she'd just been jogging. "I won't ask if you've spoken to Ella or James because I've already heard from Mrs. Talbot that you and James had an argument at work. Is that resolved?"

"What news? What's going on?" Syl asked.

"You won't believe it. Andrew Parker tried to kill himself with a bottle of pills."

"Say what?"

"You heard me correctly. That's not all of it, Syl. He wrote a letter confessing to embezzling hundreds of thousands from the firm, and it wasn't the first time."

Syl was too stunned to ask a single question, but she didn't need to. She invited Peaches to sit.

"From what I'm hearing about the letter, Paul Hope knew Parker was stealing and helped him out of the mess some years ago. Then, after all that forgiveness, Parker turned around and slept with Reba Hope. Some thanks."

"Backstabber."

"The police asked him again if he had anything to do with

Josey killing Paul Hope," Peaches said. "But he told them that he didn't need Paul dead to steal money or be with Reba."

"He said that?"

"That's what the streets of Saugerties are saying," Peaches confirmed. "Isn't this all some shit straight off the soaps?"

"What is the world coming to?" was all Syl could say. "Damn."

The two women sat in Syl's living room for a few minutes, musing over how they'd never thought their little hamlet and town would ever have so much action—and tragedy.

"I thought moving up here would get me and my crew away from all the crazy," Syl said. "Well, all of this should make Ella and James feel much better. If anyone was wondering if they had any dealings with Josey, that's closed."

"Yes," Peaches said. "Maybe I'll go over there tomorrow and check in on Ella. Anyway, looks like you were about to cook something when I came in."

"Yeah." Syl gestured for Peaches to follow her back into the kitchen. "Stay for a little while, if you're not in a rush."

"You don't have to ask me twice. I'm so tired of looking at the walls of my house, I don't know what to do." She sat at the kitchen table while Syl mixed the ground beef with bread crumbs, dried parsley, eggs, and three other spices GiGi had begged her to purchase for her cooking experiments. "My kids are complaining about the heat," Peaches said, "my husband keeps going in the bathroom with the dirty magazine, as if I can't see it tucked in the back of his shorts, and I just want to get on a bus and go somewhere."

"I miss my two, of course, but to be honest, now that the Gray situation is gone, I think I'm okay with having the house to myself awhile longer. Aside from this damn storm coming through and making us sweat, I'm doing alright. I get a lot of time to think and cry, and laugh at memories. And when the phone lines are back up and running, I'll be able to use my telephone without asking my kids' permission first."

"I know what you mean," Peaches said. "That's another thing. You know I love and miss my telephone. I especially miss Fate calling me sometimes to tease me about this thing or that thing. I know you two spoke every day, so I can't even imagine—"

Syl paused from mixing the ground beef and seasonings, and she breathed through the wave of sobbing she felt was about to come on.

"It's hard, girl," Syl said. "I swear it's hard."

"Shit, I'm sorry. I shouldn't have brought it up. You two—"

"No, it's fine, Peaches. It's fine." Syl went back to mixing. "I'm glad you came over, Peaches. I really am. I have charcoal heating out back, and you can help me eat these burgers."

Just outside Syl's back door, they sat on chairs from the kitchen and ate burgers with mustard and ketchup only. They drank ice water and had oatmeal cookies for dessert. Before packing up enough burger patties for Peaches and her family to have two each, Syl asked Peaches to sit awhile longer so they could catch up.

"I miss Fate, Peaches," Syl said. "You know he'd be here, bossing me around my own grill."

"He certainly would be," Peaches said, laughing and fanning herself.

"Every couple of hours I catch myself thinking, 'I've got to call Fate and ask him this' or 'I forgot to tell Fate that.' His nieces asked me a couple of questions I didn't know the answer to, and at least twice I almost said, 'I'll have to ask Fate.'"

"Yes," Peaches said. "I've picked up my phone a couple of times, getting ready to call and ask him something, too."

"He was truly loved around here."

"Yes, he was. By most of us, at least," Peaches said, and with her eyes she gestured toward the Whites' house. "Oh, I meant to ask you: Have you and the Whites been speaking since the funeral? And by the way, what you and Mrs. Talbot said to them, it all needed to be said. They're jealous and grieving. It's understandable, but only to a point."

Syl related that she hadn't seen much of Ella, that she had made eye contact with James at Richmont's, and that he had greeted her.

"They must be cooling off," Peaches said. Syl silently agreed. "Heard from Vincent?" Peaches asked before drinking from her glass.

"I sure haven't. Peach, I heard something today that bothered me." She told her what Javier, the electrician, had told her earlier in the day. Given that there hadn't been time for Sullivan Gray to be thoroughly questioned after he was shot, and none of his fingerprints were found in Fate's house or on the shed door, Syl couldn't help but wonder if there was a chance someone else had taken Fate's life. She almost mentioned this to Peaches, but then she remembered Gray's claim to be a disciple of Josey's, and that Fate had been killed with a knife, just as Paul Hope was.

"Well," Peaches said. "That's interesting, and I'd be all over it if we didn't know Gray did it."

"Yeah, you're right," Syl replied. But the image of what Javier had described seeing, and the memory of Vincent snapping at Hoke, fluttered around her mind like a butterfly.

After Peaches left, Syl lit candles in the kitchen and decided to organize some cabinets, all the while thinking about Fate, Gray, not having electricity, her kids wanting her to head into the city to her cousin's, her failed marriage, her mostly secret relationship with Hoke, Morgan and his parents—adopted and biological. But one thing that kept coming back around was what

Javier had confided and the fact that Gray was only assumed to be Fate's killer. Suzy's strange stares, and her odd behaviors toward Fate, could take a hike.

Then Syl's mind conjured strange questions and scenarios: What if Vincent had come up to Saugerties earlier than expected and seen Fate sneaking Blu out, then drove back to the city via some toll-free route? The what-ifs were endless, overwhelming her. She decided to lie down. Soon after, she dozed off.

At two-fifteen the following morning, Syl woke up thirsty. As she drank the glass of room-temperature water, she noticed that she hadn't put away one of the seasonings she'd used the evening before. She thought of the burgers and Peaches's visit. *Heard from Vincent?* she remembered Peaches asking.

Why haven't I heard from him? Why hasn't he returned my phone calls? I know he's grieving, but to not call back at all?

Within five minutes Syl was in her car, headed to the police station.

CHAPTER TWENTY-TWO

On any other day, Syl would've noticed that her welcome mat was in a slightly different position from how she'd left it just ten to twelve minutes prior. Its top border was no longer aligned with the doorway, but Syl was distracted by how close she had come to walking into the police station and telling them she was wary of her dead best friend's greatest love—a man they had obviously cleared of any suspicion. She had pulled over and sat thinking for a minute before deciding to go back home.

Syl went into the bathroom to brush and gargle again, and when she came out, a whiff of a very familiar scent wafted up her nose. It smelled of a man who'd been doing hard labor or exercise in the summer heat. There was a hint of a shampoo or lotion she didn't use mixed in with the sweaty odor. Syl knew she wasn't alone. It could be Vincent. It could be whatever crazy man could have killed Fate, if Gray hadn't actually done it. It could be James, coming to punish her for letting him have it outside the church after Fate's service. Just maybe, she thought, Ella had sent him to rough her up for telling Morgan the secret.

Or am I just tired, paranoid, and think I smell someone else?

Whether she was right about the smell or not, she wanted to get out of the house. She looked toward her front door and decided to make a run for it. Syl felt she *needed* to get out *right then*—even if only to go and park at the police station and sleep until the sun came up.

Just as she was about to run, she heard a hallway floorboard creak under someone's weight. Then a tall male figure appeared.

Syl opened her eyes slowly, because even while asleep she'd felt dizzy, and her head throbbed. She knew she was in a basement. Basements all smelled the same: their metallic, damp odor often mixed with the aroma of laundry powder and spilled fabric softener. But there was the smell of cigarette smoke present, too. She was lying on her side, wrists and ankles bound behind her, and her mouth was covered. When her eyes focused, she recognized that she was in a Fervent basement. Her house didn't have one, but some in Fervent did. She had been in a few of them.

There was a bright stream of daylight coming in from the curtained window at the opposite end of the basement. In the light's path sat a couch covered with what looked like piles of old clothes, boxes, rugs, and blankets. The upholstery from one of the couch's arms peeped out just enough for Syl to see that it was blue-and-beige plaid. She remembered that piece being in the Whites' living room years ago, when she first met them. If the couch wasn't confirmation enough, Morgan's yellow ten-speed bicycle, parked in the corner, was.

On the floor near her head was what first looked to her like a white rag, but it took her only a few seconds to realize it wasn't a rag at all. It was a sleeve from a terry-cloth robe, and it had brownish-burgundy spots and smears on it. Dried blood, for sure. It was the sleeve torn from Fate's robe—the same robe he was wearing when he was found dead in his shed.

My God, Syl thought. *No wonder they hadn't confronted me before now. They've been planning to kill me for telling Morgan.*

The sight of the sleeve brought on a quivering she couldn't stop.

Syl tried to scream through the tape, but no more than a forceful hum came out. With what strength she had, she rocked and sat upright, but she soon realized she was chained to a pillar in the center of the basement. Any fantasy of escape was over. She cried and rocked. Rocked and cried. Tried again and again to scream through the tape. No sounds came from upstairs. Ella and James had obviously gone out.

With every other blink Syl saw her children. GiGi's squirmy little body at just twenty or so seconds old; GiGi again, taking her first steps; RJ lying on her chest a day after the doctors cut her open, lifted him out—still in the water sack—and set him free; RJ again, at three years old, climbing a chair to get onto the kitchen counter. Her children's smiles and tantrums, their chicken pox and knee scrapes. All of it played before her as though she were watching a television show about their lives. Then another wave of dizziness came over her. Placing her face against the cold floor helped her endure it. Soon, she passed out again.

After what Syl believed to be ten to twelve hours since they'd kidnapped her, Ella came down the stairs, kicked Syl's foot a few times, and said, "Wake up and drink some of this."

It was half a glass of water. Ella ripped the tape from Syl's mouth and put the glass to her lips.

"You two are pathetic. Just kill me if you're gon' do it."

"Shut up and drink the water. I don't want you dying before I'm ready for you to."

"I won't drink. So you might as well go get a gun, knife, or whatever and kill me."

Ella produced a folded knife from her pocket and opened it.

"I'm not above torturing you, Sylvia." Then she rattled off a list of things she was willing to do that would give Syl pain. "Now drink the water." Syl had just a few gulps before Ella pulled the glass away. "Drink the rest," Ella ordered, and she put the glass back to Syl's lips. "Do you know why you're here, Sylvia?"

"Yeah. I told the truth because you wouldn't."

"Ha!" Ella seemed genuinely amused. "I suppose that's technically true. But—"

"But nothing, Ella. Fuck you."

In response to that, Ella sighed, put the tape back over Syl's mouth, and went back upstairs. Minutes later, Syl heard the couple leave. She imagined they wanted to be out and about enough to keep up appearances. With the electricity still off, hardly anyone was just sitting in their house all day.

What might have been an hour later, Syl's bladder was so full she thought it might burst. Unable to hold it any longer, she let go. Shortly thereafter, the Whites returned. She heard James say to Ella, "Let's just finish this, goddamn it. Tonight!" It came out of him sounding more like growls than words. "It ain't smart to have her in here for days."

"You forfeited your right to make any suggestions when you lost control with Fate."

"Fuck you!"

"No, fuck *you,* James!"

From what Syl could gather, the plan had been for them to kill her and Fate at the same time. She didn't yet know how they'd planned to do it.

Ella came downstairs and saw that Syl's shorts were wet.

"Damn it," Ella said, barely looking at Syl. "I can't abide the smell of urine-soaked clothes. It reminds me too much of my days in the orphanage." She summoned James to the basement, told him to pull down all the shades upstairs. Ella went up to the bathroom and ran a bath. When she came back down, she said to Syl,

"You and I are going to have a chat. And who knows? Maybe I'll change my mind and have you die by water instead of by train." The two of them escorted Syl to the bathroom—her mouth still taped over and a gun aimed at her every step of the way.

"I'll shoot if I even *feel* that you wanna make a move," James warned as they walked up the stairs to the ground level of the house. He'd obviously had a shower. She smelled that same shampoo from earlier that morning when he'd kidnapped her.

Syl wondered how they would explain away the sound of a gunshot in their house. She considered doing something just so James might drop the gun, causing it to go off. But she thought of Ella's threats of torture. Syl believed herself a strong person, but unless suffering excessive and lasting pain was required to save her children, she didn't believe she could endure it.

When they arrived at the bathroom entrance, Syl could smell the white vinegar that had been put in the bath. James handed Ella the gun and said, "You know what to do if she even looks like she's gonna try something. I'm goin' just up the road to do some pull-ups."

"Pull-ups, James?" Ella said.

"Yeah," he shot back. "Out in public where people can see me doin' my normal shit," he said. "That okay with you, *boss*? Is it?"

"Fuck off!" Ella shouted back. She released an angry sigh as James walked out.

Syl was instructed to undress slowly, get into the tub, and scrub herself with the worn washcloth Ella tossed into the water. Disrobing in front of the person who was preparing to kill her made Syl sick to her stomach.

Syl scrubbed hard and quick. Ella leaned against the counter, gun in her right hand. Then, to Syl's surprise, she said, "Take your time. There's no *big* rush." She closed the toilet lid and sat. Syl saw her shoulders slump forward just a bit. "Why, Sylvia?" Her voice was quiet, calm, and clear. "Why'd you tell Morgan they were still alive?" She snatched the tape from Syl's mouth.

Syl continued scrubbing while staring into Ella's eyes.

"He deserved to know. He was a grown man and old enough to know the truth," Syl said. She had fantasized many times in the past few days about saying those words to James and Ella. "How'd you find out I told him?"

"I learned it from Morgan," Ella said. Syl was perplexed. Then Ella stood up and pulled a small notebook from her back pocket. "He wrote *all* about it in here." Syl was astonished to see that it was not the journal from which she had snatched pages. "The day you and your kids came over, it fell out of a crate of records, but I didn't pay it much attention. I just tossed it on his dresser and kind of forgot about it until the night before the memorial walk in Cairo." Syl said nothing. "What were you trying to do? Erase me from Morgan's life? 'You have another mother, Morgan, and she's *Black,* like *me,* and not in prison like Ella.' That's what you said to my son. Isn't it, Sylvia?"

"As I've just said: he had the right to know." Tears ran down her face, but she locked eyes with Ella the whole time, knowing it could mean being shot. "I did you a favor by not telling him the moment he finished high school."

"Am I supposed to *thank* you?" Ella taunted. "You never liked James and me being parents to Morgan. You told us in soooooo many ways, soooo many times, Sylvia."

"I'll give you this: maybe I laid it on a little thick. But at least I was right about him not needing to be with *you* two." She stopped scrubbing. "It's obviously going to cost me my life, and my children will be without a mother, but it won't be in vain." She felt as though her heart might fly out of her chest and into the bathwater. "But just so you know, Morgan believed—we *all* believed—that you and James were in prison for life."

"Yeah, yeah. You thought we were guilty, too, didn't you?" Then Ella released a grunt that reminded Syl of her own labor pains.

"I don't know what you want me to say, Ella. Just shoot me, if you're gon' do it."

The electricity snapped back on, and the sounds coming from the television startled them both.

Ella stood in the doorway, keeping her eyes on Syl the whole time, gun still in hand. Ella held the weapon much like Mrs. Talbot had held hers.

"You don't know what it's like to be abandoned by the people who gave you life, do you, Sylvia?" Like a junkie, unable to decide what to do with her body, Ella moved back to the toilet seat, sat down again, and crossed one leg over the other. "I asked you a question." Syl shook her head no. There were a few beats of silence, and Syl saw Ella soften again. "Losing your parents to death after a long illness, or even a sudden death, has to be hard. I wouldn't dare suggest it isn't. But Morgan's mom and dad each held him for about five minutes. That's *it.* Can you imagine holding GiGi and RJ for only a handful of minutes, then never again?"

Just hearing her children's names made Syl want to leap from the water and take the biggest chance on life. Instead, she sat still, thinking, looking around the room, planning—just in case she might get a perfect opportunity to save herself.

Ella got up and paced a bit more, put a new piece of tape over Syl's mouth, and sat back down on the toilet lid.

"It's story time, Sylvia," she taunted. "Four days before Morgan was born, Gwinette called me. Our every-three-months talks had long ago fizzled out. So, I hadn't heard her voice in a few years, but she always sent me a birthday card in October, and the occasional postcard if she went to a new city for the first time. It was her way of letting me know she was alive, well, and thinking about me.

"I remember that phone call very well, Sylvia. It was on a Saturday morning around eleven o'clock. James and I were renting a one-bedroom apartment in Kingston at the time. He had gone down to Newburgh to help a friend of his fix up an old truck, car, or something. I knew the second I heard Gwinette's voice that she was calling for an important reason. She didn't beat around the bush. We weren't on the call more than three minutes before she said, 'Sis, will you take my baby and raise it?' I was stunned, Sylvia. 'You have a *baby*?' I asked her. I didn't know which information to address first, the fact that she had a baby or that she was asking me to take it. 'Not yet, but I'm due any day now,' she told me.

"Gwinette and Thomas were only nineteen and twenty at the time. She said she felt for the child growing inside her, but something was off with her emotions, she told me. I didn't press her to explain at the time because we'd both been abandoned as small children. I had an idea what she was thinking. 'You're not them, Gwinette,' I reminded her, but she didn't want to hear any of that. 'Ella, stop it. Please,' she said. Gwin said she and Tom weren't going to keep the baby when it came. Said they simply weren't ready. She said, 'If you, or maybe a person or couple you know and trust, can't take her, we'll put her up for adoption at the hospital. Take a day to think about it and I'll call you back this time tomorrow. Either way you decide, you're still my big sister.'

"She was *so* sure it was a girl," Ella said with a chuckle. "*So* sure.

"I told her I didn't need a day. I'd take her baby. Thinking back on it, I probably should've at least given James an opportunity to weigh in. Things would've gone my way in the end, regardless. But in that moment, I just wanted to help my orphanage sister. My once *little* orphanage sister who was offering me something very special. Gwinette said, 'Are you sure you don't want to speak to your husband?' and I said, 'You know me. If it's a choice between being a mom to your baby and *James,* there's nothing to think about. You're my *family.* That baby is my family, too.'"

At hearing this, Syl thought briefly of Clyde, the boy back home who'd been adopted by the white McLaughlins. Syl wondered if maybe Mrs. Virginia McLaughlin had made a similar promise to Clyde's mother. He had clearly turned out to be a man who cared about the rights and happiness of Black people.

"So, Gwinette and Tom were out in Chicago. Someone Tom knew had gotten them jobs, and they were renting a room in a boardinghouse. With the baby due any day, I knew I needed to get out there to her. She gave me the address where she and Tom lived. I threw some clothes in a suitcase, wrote James a note explaining that I was headed to be with Gwinette because she was having an emergency situation, that I'd call him once I got where I was headed. Then I got on the road. I left home around noon, and by nine o'clock that night, I was in Akron, Ohio. I got a motel room, got a burger and fries, showered, ate, and fell sleep. I finished the drive to Chicago the next morning.

"Gwinette's belly was so large, I wondered how she was able to stand up without help. She was quite petite. But she moved around as if she wasn't carrying a nine-pound little person inside her. I said, 'Are you afraid, Gwin?' and she said, 'Hell yeah, I'm scared.' We were at a diner. She'd said she was craving pancakes, but instead of syrup, she wanted them topped with—get ready for this, Sylvia—cottage cheese, cinnamon, and nutmeg. The waitress said, 'I'd think you were weird if your belly hadn't come through the door before you did.' It tickled me pink. Did you have strange cravings like that, Sylvia? Shake your head or nod.

"Well, I suppose most pregnant women do. I never got the opportunity. Whether it's my body or James's, I don't know. Doesn't matter anymore anyway."

It was a great wonder to Syl. Ella White, a woman who had so willingly cared for a child she hadn't birthed, a Black child her husband hadn't initially wanted around, was the same person holding another mother captive and planning to kill her, leaving her children orphaned. *Fate always said they were crazy.*

"After we ate, I dropped Gwinette back off at her apartment—rooming house, rather—and went to the motel to watch the news, read some of the paperback thriller someone had left in the drawer next to the Bible, and napped. My intentions were to meet Gwinette the next morning for a walk. The doctor at the clinic told her to do as much walking as she could, and she preferred mornings. But just a few hours after I dropped her off, a woman who lived in the rooming house called my room. 'Is this Ella? I'm calling for Lil Bit,' she said. I was not at all confused about who she was referring to. Anyway, Gwinette's labor had started and she wanted me to come and take her to the hospital."

Ella sounded like a proud grandmother. For half a second, Syl's heart warmed for her.

"Things moved along pretty slow after we got to the hospital. Her contractions were far apart and the nurse told us we may as well have waited longer to come in. But neither of us had had a baby before. We didn't know you could just wait around at home until things *really* got going. Are you listening to me, Sylvia?"

Sylvia only made eye contact with Ella, which was accepted as a yes. Syl stole more glances around the bathroom, trying to see if there was something to use as a weapon, in case she, by any stroke of God-given gumption, were to charge Ella and knock the gun from her hand.

"Good," Ella said. "I want you to hear every word of what you've taken from me. Gwinette would kill you herself, probably, if she was alive." To that, Syl furrowed her brow. "Oh, you didn't know that part, did you? You sent *my* son looking for two people who died years ago. Sylvia, you probably don't remember this, but James and I once left Morgan with the Talbots for a few days to go on a trip." Syl did remember. She had complained to Reggie that Morgan would have had more fun staying at their house. "Gwinette had passed. Lupus took her. Tom was already dead. Accident at a construction site." Ella took a heavy sigh. "How do you feel now, knowing that?"

Syl let the wave of old guilt about having told the secret pass over her as the tears ran effortlessly from her eyes. Maybe she would take it all back now, knowing that Morgan's trip had been for nothing.

"Anyway, Gwinette and I had a good time talking and laughing about funny things she'd done or said as a kid, when we were still at the orphanage. All the reminiscing took my mind off the beautiful but hard parts that were to come. And I'm not talking about watching Gwinette give birth. I'm talking about my becoming a parent to a new little person. A new little person that my husband didn't know I'd be returning with.

"Morgan was so precious. My *gosh,* he was the most precious, and the *biggest,* newborn baby I'd ever laid eyes on. An absolute angel, which you know. He never stopped being precious.

"It was very possible that my marriage would be over the moment I walked in the door with the baby. James tried to take Morgan from me once. Well, he didn't try to *take* him, exactly. But he tried like hell to get me to give Morgan up for adoption again, put him in the foster-care system down in the city, where he'd be placed in a Black home. 'We don't know anything about raisin' a Black kid.' James must've said that four million times. We were in the living room of our apartment. 'How in Christ's sake did you adopt a kid in thirteen days, anyway? I know it takes longer than that,' he yelled. He was right, but, Sylvia, I'd called someone who'd once cared for Gwinette and me like we were her own. We begged for her help, and she wired me five thousand dollars and told us to find a lawyer who wasn't 'too fancy,' as she said. Gwinette already had the names of a few she'd heard could make things happen in a snap. So, we went to one, showed him the cash, and let me tell you, Sylvia, I learned that week what people mean when they say money is power. Ten days after Morgan was born, I was his legal mother.

"Anyway, I'd laid the baby Morgan down in the center of our bed, shielding his innocence from all the stupidity I knew James would spew. 'I don't *want* to know anything about raising a Black kid,' he yelled. 'You have any idea what people will say about us? Did you take even a single moment to think about any of this, Ella? They'll call us nigger lovers!'

"I didn't move from my end of the couch. I didn't even let on to James that I'd been stunned by what he said. I sat there thinking for about four, five minutes before getting up and walking to the kitchen table. That's where I'd set my half-full bottle of Mountain Dew. I picked that thick bottle up, finished off the soda, and I threw that bottle at James's head with all the strength I had, which, in that moment, was a *lot.* He moved just in time, but he got my point. He. Got. My. Point, Sylvia. That's how much I *already* loved that baby. James and I just stared at each other. Broken glass seemed to be everywhere. James said, 'I'm sorry, Ella. I'm sorry,' or something like that.

"I gave him an ultimatum. 'If you love me, you'll love that child. Period,' I said to him. 'Make your decision *right* now.' The rest is history. He wasn't always the perfect dad to Morgan, as you well know. I told you some of that in my car all those years ago. But he did damn good with Morgan. Mostly.

"Anyway, I was taking so many risks at once. But you know what? I'd do it all over again. I'd fucking do it all over again for that child. If Gwinette was alive, had another child today, and asked me to raise it, I'd do it again." She removed the tape from Syl's lips. Gently, this time. "Be honest with me, Sylvia. Can you really sit there, after everything I've just told you, and still believe

I was less of a mother to Morgan, or loved him any less than you love your own two kids, just because he was Black and I'm white?"

Syl steadied her breathing. The sobbing had nearly suffocated her.

"No," Syl said, and she meant it.

"Look at me, Sylvia." Syl slowly turned her gaze from the water to Ella. "I would've given my life for Morgan, one million times over."

"I know," Syl said. "I hear it in your voice and see it on you. I do. I was wrong for thinking a white couple can't truly love and take good care of a Black child. Wrong for thinking you couldn't love Morgan as much as I could. I was wrong. And I'm sorry. Truly."

Ella scoffed and said, "Truly? You'll say anything *now,* hoping it'll save you."

"Then why even ask me, Ella? If you don't believe me, why ask me any questions at all? Yeah, I suppose you're right. I want to stay alive for my kids. I'm a mother. So were you. And you loved Morgan very much. I was just plain wrong."

Ella was still sitting on the toilet lid. Syl saw her forearms relax, and her grip loosed on the gun, tears flowing all the while.

Syl heard James come back inside the house. He approached the bathroom and said, "Everything alright in there, Ella? Is she finished?"

"Almost," Ella said. She instructed him to go into the living room, saying that she'd call out to him in a few minutes, once Syl was dressed again. Syl heard him walk several feet away, into their kitchen, where Syl heard him open their silverware drawer. "Have fresh tape ready when I call."

"Ella," Syl whispered. The desperation to live was revving up. Now was the time to appeal to Ella's humanity. "Listen to me. I heard you two talking about what happened to Fate. *James* might be a killer, but you aren't." At that, Ella's shoulders began to shake and she tried to muffle her sobs with the hand that didn't have a gun in it. Syl understood this particular type of crying. It was gratitude at being understood and cared for. "You don't have to go back to prison or be on the run for the rest of your life. We could call the police, or—"

Ella lifted the gun and pointed it at Syl's face. Her form was as stiff as ever. Her grip on the gun was so tight, Syl could hear the metal making adjustments.

"Don't say another word," she ordered. The crying had come to an abrupt halt, almost as if it had been a performance. But Syl knew it hadn't been. "We? There's no you and me, Sylvia. There's only James and me. I can't blame you for trying, though." Slowly, Syl leaned her back against the tub's edge, accepting that she would be dying soon. "Yeah," Ella said. "May as well let go. It's over. I know you didn't force Morgan to go to D.C., and I know you didn't cause the accident that killed him. But you gave him the information that made him want to go. For that, I cannot and will not forgive you. If RJ wasn't down south with his dad, you and I would be even already."

Ella must have been able to see that Sylvia was about to scream as loud as she could, because she said, "No no no. Don't do it. Remember all the things I could do before I let you die. I haven't forgotten. Just let go," Ella said. "You will die for your son, Sylvia. The ultimate sacrifice." Ella was so calm while talking about the imminent murder, it made Syl wonder if it would be the last thing Ella did on earth. Then Ella said as much: "But come to think of it, who knows? Maybe I'll go ahead and finish myself off after the train takes care of you. Because really, Sylvia, what do I have to look forward to?" She shrugged and whispered, "Another twenty, thirty years with James? He's a liability, as you well know." She shrugged again. "On the other hand, time heals things. There's still a chance we could be somewhat happy again."

Ella, gun pointed, tossed Syl a towel and told her to dry off. Syl dressed in the large, faded red T-shirt and sweatpants she'd seen draped over the shower curtain rod.

"Let's take her back downstairs," Ella called out to James. "I'm done talking to her, for now."

In the basement, they bound Syl's wrists and ankles with more tape. The couple went back upstairs, but they didn't shut the door firmly behind them. "I've got to run out for about an hour," Ella said.

"Where to, for fuck's *sake*?"

"Jenny from the school got into a bad wreck, and if I don't go see her, everyone will know something's off."

"No one's expecting visitors when half of Saugerties has no power, Ella. Goddamn it."

"How many times do I have to tell you they moved to Woodstock?" she scolded. "Anyway, I'll stay twenty minutes and come right back. I've got more to say to that one down there, so she'd better be very much alive and well when I get back. As a matter of fact, just come with me."

"You fuckin' kiddin' me? Come on," he barked. "What am I now? Some uncontrollable maniac killer? She'd be gone already if that was the case. You better believe it."

There was a silence; then Ella said, "You do anything to her, kill yourself right after. Because if you rob me of the chance to say all I need to say to the person who took my child from me, I will kill you, James."

"You think you're the only one's got things to say? He was my son, too, goddamn it!"

"I'm glad you feel that way."

"Fuck you."

"One hour," Ella said sternly. "I'll be back in one hour."

CHAPTER TWENTY-THREE

The time in prison had done something to James's mind. Syl couldn't imagine what Fate's final moments with James in the shed had been like.

With Syl, his eyes were wild, just as one might expect from those of a killer. Syl wondered if James had killed others in such a gruesome manner while in Vietnam.

James sat an old, rusty folding chair in front of Syl. He eased onto it as if it might crumble beneath him.

"You wanna know the last thing your best friend said before I finished him off?"

He looked at her with a sense of pleasure in his eyes as he cut off pieces of a Granny Smith apple. "This is the knife I used." He held it out toward Syl as though he expected her to examine it closely. Syl looked away and he removed the tape from her lips. This time, when she licked them for moisture, she tasted blood.

"I hope you suffer a long and painful death, James," Syl said, and she spit at him what little bit of saliva had formed in her mouth. He put the tape back over her mouth. It took a couple of attempts before he got it to stay on.

"Well, there goes us havin' a civil conversation," he said, sliding a piece of the fruit between his teeth and crunching. She would have thought the sight of food would make her hungry, but it did not. Syl glanced at him just as he winced. "Holy shit, that's a tart one, Syl!" He giggled. High-pitched. "Anyway, I guess I'll do all the talking. Your buddy said, 'I knew it would be you.'" James wiped his face with the hem of his T-shirt. "I watched him moving around his kitchen, mixing cake batter like a little ole woman or something, dancin' to his radio. He put the cake pans in the oven and went to run a fancy little bath. It was easy as pie for me to unlock his back door, Syl. Easy as pie, man. I learned how to pick a lock when I was eleven. These upstate kids don't have shit on guys like me, born and raised in the city. Anyway, that's how I got in *your* house. Picked the lock. I was planning to grab you while you were sleeping, but you made it a little easier for me by leaving out at two-somethin'. Where the hell did you go? Never mind. I don't care. At least I was able to get in your house while it was empty.

"Anyway, with Fate fillin' the tub, and hummin' some sing-song, he didn't hear a *thing.* Not a *thing.* I punched him a couple of times and dragged him out to his shed, where that noisy lawn mower of his is, and I made him sit down next to it. I told him we didn't need him spreadin' that queer disease around. He said he didn't have it, but I figured he'd catch it sooner or later. I was kinda doin' the guy a favor. Don't you think?

"I pulled out this knife and sent him on quickly. I wasn't in the mood for much more of a discussion. I'm really not all that jazzed about you still being alive right now. I wanted to kill you in your house, but Ella—" He sighed and rolled his eyes. "She wants you to go in her own planned-out, dramatic way. Anyway, I took this little knife and sent the blade straight to his heart a handful of times. Pretty quick that way, you know. He didn't suffer long, if that makes you feel any better. I'm not a fucking *monster,* Syl. I wanted it over with. In Nam, we killed quickly. No time for torture, unless we needed information. I didn't need any information from Fate. He'd given plenty in that fuckin' testimony he gave when I was on trial."

Just then, the worn tape fell from Syl's mouth. He didn't move to put it back on.

"Just do it, James, and shut up," Syl said, her head leaning against the pillar. It was then that she realized Hoke had never told her exactly what he'd seen in Fate's shed. He had only said that there was lots of blood.

"Can't do that," he said before continuing his speech. He spoke as though he were just talking to some of the men at Aco about a baseball game he'd watched the previous night. "Anyway, I didn't know how to speak Vietnamese, so." He cut and ate another chunk of the apple. "*Then* I took Fate's heart, because that's what Josey did, and if Gray was a real follower, it's what he would've done. Right?"

"You *are* a fucking monster," Syl said. "Killed a person for annoying you several years ago?"

"Several *years* ago? Come on, Syl. He disrespected me over and over. Had it coming," he said with a shrug. "For years that freak had it comin'. He wasn't the angel yous made him out to be, either. But I'm sure you know he wasn't a saint. Don't you? Come on, be honest."

"What are you *talking* about, you fucking psycho?" Syl asked, though it didn't matter a great deal. By then, she halfway wanted him to just put the blade of the knife into her heart, since Ella had already told her she'd be dead soon. Their telephone rang, but he ignored it.

"He wasn't faithful to that other fancy fruitcake he was dating all those years. He had a whole other thing going with another sissy that works at the hospital. I don't know his name, of course, but I'd seen them together a *lot*. Fate was a cheater."

Syl almost asked him why he'd care about Fate's love life, but instead she said, "You know what, James?" Tears dripped from her chin and onto the red T-shirt. "I should've hated you when your temper caused me to need stitches. That toy could've blinded me in one eye. But I guess my heart was saving the hate up. Now I really and truly hate you—and Ella."

James finished chewing what was in his mouth, swallowed, and said, "I've long hated you, Fate, and most of these so-called *good* people here in Fervent. None of you know what a good person is. I fought for my country. Took out people who'd see America *fall. I'm* the good person in this room, in this hamlet."

The fact that he believed himself to be good, and the rest of them bad, told Syl all she needed to know about who James was and had always been. He was delusional.

"So, none of this is 'bout your love for Morgan, is it?" Syl asked.

James stared down at his feet for a few seconds. "I loved the kid," he said. "I *grew* to love the kid, mostly because Ella loved him so much and I wanted to protect anything that made her happy. But did I want to raise a Black child? Shit no, I didn't, Syl. Would you want to raise a *white* kid?" Syl didn't say anything, but she knew her answer. She didn't think he really wanted a response. "I asked you a question."

"Fuck you and your questions, James."

He let out another of his high-pitched giggles. "Then you understand," James said.

"I'd raise *any* child better than you and Ella ever could," Syl shot back.

"I doubt that, Syl, but if you say so." There was a minute of silence between them. "Ella loved Morgan a hundred times more than she loves me. You know that, right? I was jealous of that. So, fuck yeah, I was hard on the boy. Loved him, but I was tough on him because I wanted Ella to see his weaknesses and to see how strong *I* was. I wanted to remind her that I, *I* was and always would be her protector. A white man. Not him. A Black boy. But it was stupid. All it did was make her more protective of him and irritable with me. Made her love him even more. So, I cooled out on him. When I chilled out, I could tell Ella's old love and appreciation for me came back."

"When are we goin' to the train for y'all to kill me, James? Since you're too scared of Ella to just do it here."

"Listen," he said, sitting back in the chair. "I don't know. Ella's in charge of all that."

Syl began to sob again.

"Didn't know she had it in her, did you, Syl?" He laughed. "Ella's something else. We're both crazy like that. We love hard and hate even harder. My dad walked out on my mother and me when I was ten, and never sent us so much as a five-dollar bill to buy food. Ella's mom dropped her off at a church and married some guy. So, yeah, we've got a lot of love in our hearts, but we're two hurt motherfuckers, too. So, when someone fucks with what good we *do* have, we don't take it lightly."

"Sounds like *you* don't really want me dead," Syl said. "Let me go and my kids and I swear you'll never see or hear from us again."

"Nope. No can do."

"Then take me somewhere and just shoot me, James. I don't want to die the way Ella's planned it. My kids won't be able to handle knowing I died that way."

"You know where my loyalty lies, Syl. Come on. Ella wants revenge, and I want her to be happy. Nothin' personal. Well, it's a little personal, I guess. I don't much like you. But even if it was the mailman who told Morgan the secret, I'd be sitting here talkin' to him instead of you."

Syl scoffed and said, "Loyalty. Ella doesn't want to be with you, stupid."

"What?"

"She's going to kill herself after I'm dead," Syl blurted out. "She said so. She's going to kill herself after the train hits me. She might kill *you* before that. If you won't let me go, please just shoot me and bury me somewhere. Please."

Just then, a car door closed outside.

CHAPTER TWENTY-FOUR

The footsteps above were hard and fast, as though they might be running from someone.

"James!" Ella shouted down the stairs. "Come up here, quickly!" He put fresh tape over Syl's mouth. Two pieces. "Hurry up!" she yelled.

James did not rush up the stairs, and he left the basement door wide open.

"You planning on offin' yourself after she's dead?" he asked once he reached the landing.

"What?"

"Is that what you told her, Ella?" James asked. Syl wondered if he was about to cry. The pitch of his voice nearly rose to that of the giggle.

"Let go of my arm, right now," Ella growled. Syl could tell she was making an effort not to yell. But why? Was someone in the yard?

"You plan on leavin' me high and dry, don't you?"

"Damn it, James, no. We don't have time for this now. Talbot's walking this way."

At that, it was like he'd forgotten everything he and Ella had just said. "Fuck! Fuck!"

"Shhhhhhh. Go put Sylvia in the pump room. Make sure she's tied up and cover her mouth well."

"Fuck, fuck, fuck," he said, running down the basement steps. He hoisted Syl up, took her to their pump room, which was below the living room, and closed the door. When Syl leaned her back against the wall, something sharp scraped her, stinging her badly. She breathed through the pain. Syl heard James and Ella scurrying around, likely making sure everything looked as normal as possible. Then it sounded like James hurried into the bathroom and ran the water.

Though it was faint, Syl heard the knock at the front door.

"Hi, Mrs. Talbot," Ella said. All the sounds were muffled. "I know we're due for a serious talk, but can it wait? Please. I'm busy and—"

"I'm not here to argue," Mrs. Talbot said. "I promise. I have something very important to tell you. Very important." Syl heard the squeak of the Whites' screen door, which meant that either Mrs. Talbot had pushed her way in or Ella had stepped aside and let her in.

"Hi, Mrs. T," James said.

Mrs. Talbot returned his greeting. "Before I start, have you two seen Syl? Last night or today?

"We saw her get in a taxi last night. Had a little suitcase with her. Must be going to where her kids are."

"Really? That's odd," Syl heard Mrs. Talbot say. "Are you alright, James? Your face is nearly beet red. Is it a rash?"

"No, ma'am. I'm fine. I was just moving some stuff around in the other room. This one's got me reorganizing, since we're both home from work."

"I see," Mrs. Talbot said. "Anyway, Syl usually lets me know when she's traveling—even if it's just down to the city to see her relatives. She didn't tell Hoke, either. He called me looking for her. He's out of town."

"Why would she tell Hoke?" Ella asked. Syl figured Mrs. Talbot must have given her a sheepish look because Ella then said, "Oh, I see. Well, they're both single."

"Yes, they absolutely are," Mrs. Talbot said.

Syl heard Mrs. Talbot say something about the electricians and telephone company being in Fervent. Just then, she felt moisture in the spot where her back had scraped the wall. Whatever she had leaned against had cut her. She shifted her body around to face the wall, and with her fingers, she found the rough edge of something metal.

Syl dragged the tape that held her wrists together against the sharp point that had cut her back. She did it over and over until the tape gave way. With her hands now available to her, she gently removed the tape from over her mouth and slid quietly to the pump room's doorknob to see if it was unlocked. *There is a God,* she thought, discovering that it was. She paused to listen to what was going on upstairs. Next, she would need to free her ankles.

"What was it you needed to tell us, Mrs. Talbot?" Ella asked.

"May I ask you two to sit?" Syl heard a few footsteps. They must have honored Mrs. Talbot's request.

Syl opened the door enough to let in light, and that's when she saw the old, cracked shell of a Bic pen. It lay in a groove between the wall and the cement floor, half covered in dust and other debris.

With the pen's shell, Syl dug into the tape wrapped around her ankles, scraping one of them accidentally. The pain nearly made her yell. She peeled the tape away as gently as possible. She didn't want to wince or make any other sounds. Pushing the door open had been risky enough.

"This sounds heavy, Mrs. Talbot. I don't know that today is the right day for it. I—"

"Ella, dear, there will never be a *right* time to have this conversation," Mrs. Talbot said. "But if there is, it's now." There was a brief silence. Then Mrs. Talbot began coughing.

"Go on," Ella said.

"I care very much for the two of you," Mrs. Talbot said. "Always have. You two haven't always been easy to defend, but for years, Grant and I did, even when you, James, caused people physical harm."

With tape dangling from her ankles, Syl tiptoed to the wall of shelves, where an avocado-green fishing box sat. It was closed, and the latch was fastened. Opening it would certainly make sounds. But the open toolbox sitting on the shelf under it would not. Syl lifted a long, weathered, but sharp flathead screwdriver with both hands, as though it were a rare jewel. With stealth she didn't know was possible, she made her way to the cement stairs.

"Now that you two are back, people want you to thrive and be happy. But this discord you seem so determined to sow with our neighbors has to stop. It simply must stop."

"Mrs. T," James began. We—"

"No," Mrs. Talbot said. "Listen. This anger you have toward people, it's unreasonable. No one here caused any of that awfulness with Hope to happen to you. No one but yourselves. You have to face that."

Syl reached the top of the steps, and through the crack of the door, she saw where James, Ella, and Mrs. Talbot were sitting. James was the only one with his back to the basement door. As Syl had hoped, Mrs. Talbot was wearing her light jacket, which meant she was carrying her gun. There was no sign of the Whites' gun.

"And you won't like this part, but it is not Syl's, nor was it Fate's, fault that Morgan leaned on them and grew closer to them while you were away. I understand the envy you two must feel about that. But you have to let it go, eventually."

"We *thanked* Syl," Ella shot back.

"Yes, but James isn't speaking to Syl at Aco. And you snapped at Fate twice in one week, I'm told. It's a lot, Ella. With all this community has been through, you two and the Hopes, then going to prison, Grant dying, then Morgan, then Fate murdered by a psycho. We can't have you two causing *more* hurt. Not for yourselves or anyone else. If you can't do it for me, your other neighbors, or yourselves, if you can't manage the easy favor of being civil, maybe it's best you two consider selling and moving. You'd fetch a profit in today's market."

James stood to his feet.

"Who the *fuck* do you think you are, ole lady?" he shouted. Ella remained seated and didn't interject.

"This is what I mean," Mrs. Talbot said. She, too, stood up. "I'll go now."

"No, you won't, because now you've really pissed me the fuck off. Tellin' me and my wife to leave our home? You've *always* judged us two. I oughta knock you into next week." He punched the wall he was standing next to. Syl waited to see him recoil with pain, but he didn't. She knew she would have to make her move soon. Just then, Mrs. Talbot opened her jacket, pulled her gun from its holster, and pointed it at James.

"Stay where you are, James," Mrs. Talbot said, her voice trembling. "Both of you keep still!" The smirk on Ella's face disappeared, confirming for Syl that Ella must have put her own gun away.

James didn't obey the orders. He took a step closer to Mrs. Talbot.

Syl turned the corner, screwdriver clenched tight in her right hand, and ran straight into James's back.

"James!" Ella screamed.

"Syl?" Mrs. Talbot said.

Though James hadn't seemed to feel the tool enter the center of his back, he dropped to the floor, his eyes wide. Ella started to run to him.

"Don't move!" Mrs. Talbot said. "I'll put a bullet in you, so help me!"

Ella wailed from the couch.

Syl, breathing heavily, stepped away from James. He just stared up at her.

"You bitch! My back—oh God, my back! I can't feel my legs!" Whether he was feeling any pain or not, Syl couldn't be sure. He could not move anything below his waist. Within a handful of seconds, he was calling her every possible epithet.

"I should've gotten you when I had the chance," James said. "You nig—"

Syl kicked James in the face with her shoeless foot, causing Ella to scream.

"Goddamn murdering piece of shit!" Syl shouted at him, feeling pain herself now. She thought she might have broken a toe. James was lying still and silent, his eyes closed. Syl turned toward Ella and said, "You two might be *worse* than Josey. You killed a man you knew! And were about to do it again. Neither of you are fit to be anybody's parents—Black or white."

"Syl, honey, are you hurt anywhere?" Mrs. Talbot asked, her gun still aimed at Ella. Syl heard the question but didn't reply. Sharp pains consumed her foot, but she glared at James, wanting to kick him over and over. Blood was coming from his nose. "Syl, sweetheart, go over to the phone and see if it's working." Syl heard that, too, but she didn't move. If anyone had asked her how long she stood there, looking down at James, she wouldn't have been able to tell them.

Mrs. Talbot, with her gun still pointed at Ella, walked slowly across the room to their telephone. With one hand, she placed a call and asked the person on the other end to send officers and an ambulance.

"I've just shot a kidnapper, and I have his accomplice at gunpoint," she said to the operator. She gave the address. "They may have committed a murder a couple of weeks ago, too. Tell the police to come quickly. And send as many as you can."

CHAPTER TWENTY-FIVE

James was rushed into surgery. Mrs. Talbot heard from a nurse she knew that he was unlikely to walk without assistance again. One week later, Ella was transferred from the county jail back to Bedford Hills. James would be sent back to Attica after recovering sufficiently.

Ella, a lawyer predicted to Syl, would likely be sentenced to at least forty years in prison without the possibility of early release. James would never be released.

In the weeks after Syl's rescue, Mrs. Talbot and other neighbors gently scolded her for not having told them that the Whites were a looming threat.

"I understand why you told Morgan about his blood parents," Peaches said. "I wouldn't have judged you one bit. Don't *ever* keep something like this from us again. Those two could've *killed* you and we wouldn't know a *thing*." Mrs. Talbot, Gloryanne, and Nel were also there at Syl's house, visiting and lining up to lecture her. And Syl thought that if she had to hear one more person say, "You didn't put Morgan on that train, Syl. His death isn't your fault," she would lose her mind.

By the end of the summer, the bank had taken possession of the Whites' property. It was sold at auction, and Mrs. Talbot won the bidding. Almost everyone in Fervent thought it was strange that she'd want their house, but Mrs. Talbot had plans she wasn't sharing.

A couple of months later, on Thanksgiving Day, Syl asked Mrs. Talbot what she was going to do with the Whites' lot. They were in Syl's kitchen.

"I'm going to have the house demolished in the spring."

"Then what?" Hoke asked, sitting next to Syl, holding her hand.

"I'm thinking a pool or maybe just a little park with some trees, two gazebos, for Fervent residents only—and our guests, of course. That's something Fate would've liked to have here, I believe."

"Yeah, he would've," Syl said.

"Yeah," Hoke said. "Permits won't be easy, though."

"Yes, they will," Mrs. Talbot said. "Do you know who I am?" They chuckled. "We'll come up with a name for it that honors Morgan and Fate."

RJ came into the kitchen to fix himself a second plate of food. He and GiGi were eating in the living room while watching TV.

"I'm moving to Atlanta after I graduate," he said. "This place has bad juju."

From the other room, GiGi yelled, "You're not moving to Georgia. You're too much of a momma's boy."

GiGi had received an early acceptance offer from Bard College, which was her top choice—in remembrance of Fate.

"Syl, have you heard from Fate's nieces?" Mrs. Talbot asked.

"Renee called this morning and asked me to tell you all hello," Syl reported. "They plan to come up and empty his house out in April and put it up for rent."

"That's smart," Mrs. Talbot said. "There's a new factory coming this way. Food, I'm told. So, they'll have renters for sure. Any words from Vincent?"

"He's called a couple of times," Syl said. "But I can't get him to come and visit me."

"We don't blame him, though," Hoke chimed in. "Bad memories. First thinking your loved one was taken from you by a stranger, then finding out that it was a neighbor all along? Terrible."

"Mmmm," Mrs. Talbot hummed as she shook her head. "I'm so glad Gray didn't actually get a chance to take any lives."

After Ella and James were arrested, the local news stations and papers brought up the fact that Mrs. Downing had heard Gray tell her husband, "You would've been my worse." But Mr. Downing clarified that Gray had actually said, "You would've been my first." Gray had been slipping into unconsciousness, and his speech was slurred.

"Then there's the guilt Vincent probably feels," Mrs. Talbot added. "Guilt over his sneaking around. I mean, I know he and Fate both had other lovers, but Vincent had been coming up here to see that professor for *months* without Fate knowing a thing about it."

In the days that followed James and Ella's most recent arrest, Mrs. Talbot had heard from her sources that Vincent had been seeing a closeted professor who lived in Woodstock. In fact, Vincent had been in Woodstock the night Fate was murdered. When he'd knocked on Syl's door on that awful morning, he had only been pretending to have just arrived from Manhattan. Vincent had been with his other lover, and they'd had a small gathering. Seven people were able to verify his whereabouts. They had partied into the wee hours of that morning.

"You think Fate would've cared all that much?" Hoke asked.

"It's hard to say," Syl replied. "Fate was full of surprises."

"And love," Mrs. Talbot said.

"And love," Syl said.

ACKNOWLEDGMENTS

I'd first like to thank my readers. Your kind and supportive emails and DMs are invaluable. I'm also incredibly grateful to booksellers and Bookstagrammers for showing writers so much love.

To my agent, PJ Mark of Janklow & Nesbit: A million different "Thank You!" cards can't express how thankful I am to you for all you do for me, my work, and many writers I've met. I could go on and on here, but I'll leave it at this: Thank you so very much.

To my editor, Nicole Counts: Thank you for believing in this project and taking a chance on it and me. Much gratitude to Victory Matsui for stepping in to help with editing while Nicole was on leave. To Oma Beharry, Loren Noveck, Bonnie Thompson, publicity, marketing, and everyone at One World: I appreciate all your hard work. I'm blown away by all you do for writers. It doesn't go unnoticed.

I very much enjoy the time I spend with my friends who are writers, and I want my friends who aren't writers to know that they also provide me with an immense amount of love, care, laughs, and inspiration. I can only hope I do the same for them.

I'm grateful for my momma's sisters. They are simply wonderful.

ABOUT THE AUTHOR

DE'SHAWN CHARLES WINSLOW is the author of *In West Mills,* a Center for Fiction First Novel Prize winner, an American Book Award recipient, a Willie Morris Award for Southern Fiction winner, and a Los Angeles Times Book Prize, Lambda Literary Award, and Publishing Triangle Award finalist. He was born and raised in Elizabeth City, North Carolina, and graduated from the Iowa Writers' Workshop.

deshawncharleswinslow.com

Instagram: @deshawncharleswinslow